A Dark S⌐

Edited by

Roo B. Doo

and

H.K. Hillman

The Twentieth Underdog Anthology
from Leg Iron Books

Spring 2023

Disclaimer

These stories are works of fiction. Characters, names, places and incidents are either the product of the authors' imaginations or are used in a fictitious context. Any resemblance to any persons, living or dead, or to any events or locales is entirely coincidental. If any of the events described have really happened to you then I'm afraid that's your own problem.

Copyright notice

LEG IRON BOOKS

https://legironbooks.co.uk/

Front cover image © H. K. Hillman, 2023

ISBN: 9798393272395

Contents

Foreword

H. K. Hillman

Spring is in the air, as the saying goes. Normally a pretty pleasant time of year, but after the lunacy and fakery of the last three years, it doesn't feel quite the same.

This year, it seems the 'spring' in question is a heavy, dirty, rusty one that is about to come crashing down on us all only to bounce back up and come crashing down again. Repeatedly.

At least the daffodils are blooming. There is still something to smile about. For now.

The future, at this time, does not look good. I won't go into details here but the mood in this latest resurgence of the world is darker than I have ever known. This darkness is reflected in most of the stories in this anthology – normally the most light hearted of the three we put out each year. I am left to wonder how dark the stories will be in the next volume, the Halloween one.

My own stories are of course generally dark anyway so I doubt anyone will notice any difference in mine.

It's not all doom and gloom, even though that is generally my default position and has been for a very long time now. We have a new author to welcome to the Underdog Anthologies. Tarquin Sutherland opens this book with a poem.

A dark one.

What Happens?

Tarquin Sutherland

What happens when discourse dissipates
...and fair hands are replaced with foul?
What happens if debate disintegrates
...and a grin gets replaced with a growl?
What happens where life's legitimacy
...is wiped clean - like a slate, with a cloth?
And what happens should Liberty be snatched away?
...will The People all then vent their wrath?

What happens when freedom flounders
...and The State becomes foe and not friend?
What happens if speech becomes bounded
...self-expression an act to offend?
What happens where censors censure
...and the chains exist only in brains?
And what happens should all of our hope then be lost
...just how does one confront the insane?

What happens when history itself becomes moot
...and one's birthright is stolen away?
What happens if lies are allowed to take root
...and officialdom bent to betray?
What happens where books are both buried and burned
...and The Dead, themselves - held to account?
And what happens should anger reach boiling point
...and all argument too steep to surmount?

What happens when conflict comes easy
...and all dreams become waking nightmare?
What happens if we're forced to watch kith and then kin
...become broken and left in despair?
What happens where men are left with little choice
...and self sacrifice seems easy for some?
Should that happen shall we all then lay our lives on that line
...and push up poppies for the generations to come?

Bedding into Business

Adam D. Stones

Around the Sun Bar, Copernicus Station – 2323

Condensation ran down the side of a mostly full, second pint of beer, leaving tracks through the more stable water drops. Helena Tyche watched them wind their way down, trying to guess which direction the drops would snake next. There wasn't much else to watch in the small booth. The bar was mostly empty, though only vague shapes could be seen though the constant cascade of water which formed the privacy screen, muting the music from the main section. Her sister, Ophelia, slouched on the bench next to her, far less patiently. Three beers down and working steadily on the fourth, Ophelia was naturally a faster drinker but had a correspondingly higher tolerance.

"We should just go, Hels. They aren't coming."

"We wait. They'll be here." Helena responded, sounding more convinced than she actually was.

"Yeah, right. They were supposed to be here an hour and a half ago. How long should we wait?"

Helena didn't respond. She didn't want to say that they didn't have a choice, that they didn't have any money left, could barely afford to buy food for tomorrow, never mind refuel the ship for a journey to another station or planet. The truth was too painful, too depressing. Failure was never easy to admit and this was complete ruination. If this meeting didn't pan out, they would have to sell their ship, *Jackdaw*. That would break her sister's heart, Helena knew. The *Jackdaw*, which they affectionately called *Jackie*, was more than a home. It symbolised their hard-won freedom from slavery, the ability to go where they wanted, to do as they pleased. What they would do after selling *Jackie* would be a mystery. Copernicus Station wasn't exactly awash with job opportunities, at least, not ones that were enticing or legal.

"If they aren't here by the time I've finished my drink, we should go." Ophelia said, taking a mouthful of beer and placing her glass down deliberately to emphasise the point. There wasn't much left in the glass.

"You don't want to hang around for karaoke again this evening? You sure made an impression a couple of days ago…" Helena smirked, changing the subject in a transparent distraction attempt.

Ophelia shuddered, comically exaggerated.

"God, No! I can't believe you let me sing. It was such a cheesy song and I was barely able to stand. I'm surprised they let me back in after that crime against humanity."

"It was the duet that really cemented it in everybody's mind…"

"What duet? I don't remember a duet! With who?" Ophelia asked confusion furrowing her features.

"The sexy duet. With that guy who kept trying to buy you drinks all evening. The chunky one with a strange odour and slightly greasy skin."

"Gross!" Ophelia dry heaved comically. "Why didn't you stop me!?!"

"And miss out on all that free entertainment? Not a chance!" Helena giggled mercilessly at her sister's mortification. "Besides, it isn't like you tried to bring him home. You never bring anyone home."

"We'll definitely go after this drink." A mortified Ophelia said, blushing.

"We'll go when I've finished mine." Helena asserted.

Ophelia wasn't satisfied.

"*Pfft.* You're nursing that far too much. Get yourself on the outside of it and we can go back to *Jackie.* I want to hide under my duvet."

"And do what? We don't have a cargo or a job or anything!" Helena paused, registering Ophelia's sentence. "Get myself on the outside of it?" she glanced at Ophelia, raising a questioning eyebrow.

Ophelia grinned, shuffling herself a little more upright.

"Yeah, I heard someone say it the other day. Quite a fun little phrase, right?"

Helena smiled, glad of the levity. The merriment was short lived as the water screen split apart, allowing entry of loud music and a smart looking woman sporting a rather flattering suit cut to emphasise her slender figure. She entered the booth, shimmying along until level with the sisters. A waitress came through the opening, placing a large wine glass filled with sangria in front of the business lady before retreating.

"Can I get two more beers?" Ophelia shouted after the waitress as the curtain closed, cutting off the music.

The two parties sat sizing each other up. The sisters were unsure of what to make of the business-woman. Her suit was clearly custom made and looked like it cost more than their ship was worth. Ophelia couldn't stop staring at her beautiful, smooth features and pale skin, indicating a history lacking any manual labour or harsh environments. Office based, most likely station born and never set foot on a planet, Helena thought. Contrary to the rest of the smart appearance, her hairstyle was rather unique. Shoulder length, slicked back, straight hair, dyed an unnaturally dark black with two blue streaks running from front to back. Both sister's nostrils were assailed with a strong scent of lilies with an undercurrent of excessive money.

Poorly disguised doubt was etched on the smooth face as the lady took in the sisters. Ophelia at least looked presentable. Tight jeans and raised heel boots, while a form fitting t-shirt and short jacket emphasised her athletic figure well. Helena, by comparison was in her standard loose-fitting utility suit, pens and small tools chaotically jammed into pockets, having not had time to change after the message came over the net asking to meet immediately, phrased in a manner that wasn't really asking. There had barely been time to wipe Teflon-based oil from her hands before grabbing her own jacket and Ophelia. To then be made to sit for ninety minutes was just frustrating, she could have had a shower and changed…

"The Misses Tyche. Helen and Ophelia, I presume." The business woman said. A statement more than a question.

"Helena." Helena corrected.

"If you say so." The smartly dressed woman dismissed the correction, an air of disinterest emanating from her body language.

"What can we do for you, Miss...?" Helena asked, leaving the question hanging in the air.

"Drayton. Tina Drayton."

"What can we do for you Miss. Drayton?"

Helena watched as the smartly dressed woman took a mouthful of sangria, grimacing before swallowing.

"God, this bar is awful." She said, placing the glass gently back on the table.

Helena could see Ophelia frowning out of the corner of her eye, taking umbrage. The *Around the Sun* bar wasn't exactly a high-class establishment, but the sisters liked it for the atmosphere it provided and the cheap drink offers suitable for their exceedingly meagre budget.

"If it's so bad, why did you choose to meet here?" Ophelia asked pointedly. Helena nudged her slightly with her elbow. Tina didn't respond immediately, taking a mini-tablet from her pocket and turning it on. After tapping through a few menu screens, she placed the tablet in front of her, ready to make notes.

"I think you would stand out in the establishments I usually frequent. And I doubt you could afford the bill either." Tina finally responded, barely glancing at Ophelia.

"So, what can we do for you, Miss Drayton?" Helena said quickly, forestalling any further response from her sister.

"I have a client who needs a small package moving discreetly, reliably and urgently. Your ship is reputed to be fast..."

"The fastest!" Ophelia boasted. Tina raised a finely maintained eyebrow.

"…quite." Reading from her screen, she continued. "The *Jackdaw*. A small *Jackdaw* class ship, last one to be flying. Low detection profile, capable of high-g manoeuvres, some weapon capacity. Crewed by two sisters with one small child on board, approximate age two. You also happen to be available at short notice. There aren't many ships available at the moment capable of fulfilling our… needs. You come highly recommended. In appreciation of this, you will receive standard market shipping rates plus ten percent. Are you interested?"

Helena didn't pause to consider, desperation causing her to focus on the potential payday ahead. She knew that if she didn't try to haggle though, it would raise suspicions.

"We're interested. Payment up front. Commercial rate plus twenty percent. Consumables and incidentals in addition to the fee."

"Hang on, Hels." Ophelia interrupted. "Who is your client? What are we delivering? How do you know all this about us? Come to think of it, who are you? And who recommended us?"

Helena put a hand on her leg under the table quietening her sister. Ophelia could only watch as the two negotiated the terms, head turning back and forth as if watching a tennis match. Tina ignored the interruption, focussing on Helena. "Rate plus twelve. Consumables are part of the fee, any *relevant* incidentals will be covered. Half in advance, half on delivery."

"Rate plus fifteen." Helena countered. "Half and half. Relevant incidentals. Full tanks of fuel in advance, anything excess we keep, other consumables covered by us."

"Rate plus thirteen. Other terms acceptable."

"Now both of you wait just a damn minute!" Ophelia snapped. "There's two of us on that ship and, since I'm the one who can fly her, you'll damn well answer my questions or we won't be going anywhere any time soon."

Tina appeared slightly surprised at the outburst before recovering her poker face.

"Oh, I'm sorry. Allow me to introduce myself." She didn't sound sorry at all, more fed up with the whole affair. Her bored tone echoed off the walls in an irritating harmonic. "Tina Drayton. Chief Executive of Drayton Intermediaries. We act as intermediaries for people who need things moving in a more, ah, discreet manner. The sort of people who don't like questions." She paused, the statement hanging in the air for emphasis, before continuing. "It's my business to know who and what ships are docked where, what they can do and the crew capabilities. As to who my client is and what you're delivering, these are matters for discretion. You should know better than to ask, really. It betrays your amateur status."

"Amateur? Ha!" Ophelia scoffed, picking herself up to sit upright. "We've been flying for thirteen years. We know what we're doing. I can understand not wanting to tell us who your client is, but the ship isn't flying anywhere unless we know exactly what we're carrying. Is it explosive? Radioactive? Does it require cryonics or a strict temperature regime? Will it be damaged by high-g manoeuvres? Or worse explode? I assume it isn't legal where we're taking it, or if it is, that there would be some import duties. Which means we'd be on the hook for tax evasion or worse. So either you tell us what you want us to carry, or we walk. Also, if it's a small item, we'll need another cargo to fill the hold. Ships like ours don't fly empty directly between ports. That would attract the attention of the authorities and make it more likely they would look hard for something."

Tina, unused to being spoken to in such an impertinent manner, stared at Ophelia, reappraising the pilot. She took in the form fitting attire and short, mousy hair, closely cropped into a crew cut for ease of maintenance in low gravity. An unassuming appearance, indistinct and easy to pass over, yet hiding resolve and intelligence. Picking up her less-than-satisfactory sangria, Tina drank some while maintaining eye contact with Ophelia.

"You're smarter than you look." Tina said, tipping her glass in a salute. Ophelia couldn't tell if she was being serious or mocking. Either way, it was something of a backhanded compliment.

"Thanks. It's compliments like that which make life worth living." The tone could have cut glass.

"Snark as well." Tina's raised eyebrow barely made a crinkle in her porcelain smooth skin.

"My sister is correct. We will need to know the basics about what we're carrying to be able to ensure delivery intact, as well as the destination. Beyond what we need to know, the specifics can be left out." Helena said, attempting to wrestle the conversation back onto a more diplomatic track before her sister could start an argument costing them the contract. The smart business woman barely looked at her before turning her head back to Ophelia.

"It's inert. Basically a data storage device. Portable on a person. No special requirements. So tell me, what does make life worth living?"

"Flying. There's nothing like it. Whether you're coasting through the vast blackness, dodging asteroids in the belt or ripping down the canyons of Ganymede, you're in control. Nobody to tell you where to go, what to do." Her voice trailed off, eyes becoming distant, "It's pure freedom," she added, barely above a whisper.

"I know what you mean. Being beholden to no-one. To choose what you do and when. There's no better feeling."

"Aren't you based here on the station? Doesn't that limit your freedom?" Ophelia asked, earning herself a kick under the table from her sister. If Tina found the question impertinent, she didn't show any sign of it, happily responding.

"Not at all, Ophelia. Can I call you Ophelia?" She didn't pause for an answer. "There are many different types of freedom, each with its own benefits and limitations. You can go anywhere you want, experience thrilling flights and not become chained to one place. However, your financial situation is a little, precarious, shall we say? You can't know for sure when your next contract is coming or how lucrative it will be. I on the other hand, don't have to worry about such things. Running my successful business, I have regular contracts in addition to ad-hoc dealings such as this. It means I can afford whatever I want, do whatever I want, whenever I want. The price of which is living in one place, but to me that isn't a large cost. I was born here and I'm happy to stay here. Though 'ripping down the canyons of Ganymede' sounds exhilarating. I'd love to hear more about that sometime." Tina paused, staring wistfully at her glass, which she raised in a toast.

"To freedom. In all its many forms." Tina clinked glasses with Ophelia, who then bumped her tankard into Helena's. Helena went to toast with Tina, but was a little put out to find her already drinking.

"We can leave in three days." Helena said.

"Not sooner? My client *is* waiting for the delivery." Tina queried, eyes boring through the mechanic.

"No. We're waiting on some parts to be fabbed. Then we need to fit and test them. Plus, then we need to load the decoy cargo." Helena replied.

"That's somewhat disappointing. My client was hoping it would be sooner."

"My sister is an excellent mechanic. Keeps our old *Jackie* floating through the void and the engines burning right. If she says it's going to be three days, it'll be three days." Ophelia interjected.

Tina's gaze slipped back to Ophelia, eyeing her up and down. "Although, I guess a few days wait could be... tolerable..." The statement hung in the air, laden with suggestion.

"Anything to make the wait tolerable." Ophelia smirked, taking Helena's beer without asking and downing a third of it without breaking eye contact with Tina. Electric feeling flowed between the two women, anticipation sending tingling sensations coursing through the nerves. Helena blinked, usually she was the one doing the customer relations. Her sister lived for flying and in all their years of flying, had paid scant attention to the financial or social aspects of contracts. For some unfathomable reason, she found herself on the outside of this deal, looking in as a bystander.

"If the terms are acceptable, we can sign now and you can send the particulars over?" Helena asked. Tina tapped on the pad a few times and pushed her finger onto the inbuilt scanner. A single beep indicated acceptance of the fingerprint and the tablet slid unceremoniously over. Helena pushed her own finger down on the small reader until the same beep sound reverberated through the booth. As her finger came up, she was mortified to realise she had left a small oily fingerprint on the obviously expensive tablet. Tina picked it up without looking and placed it back in her pocket, focussed on Ophelia.

"Now that business is done, I'd love to hear about Ganymede. Or any other exciting tales you have. I'm sure you have plenty."

"You said this place was awful. You want to hang around here longer?" Helena asked, eager to get back to the *Jackdaw* and resume her work. Tina didn't even look at her, kept her attention on Ophelia.

"Actually, I was thinking we could go somewhere else. Somewhere with better drinks." Tina said, a slightest hint of bashfulness sneaking through her controlled composure.

"Where did you have in mind? I can't afford any of your swanky establishments. Heck, I can barely afford this place." Ophelia asked.

"I was thinking of my place, actually." Tina explained, smirking coyly.

Ophelia sat back, sizing up the svelte woman sat across from her. Tingles of excitement were pawing at the extremity of her awareness, she was very aware of the perfume the woman was wearing – lilies with a hint of jasmine that she hadn't noticed before. In all their years of flying, Ophelia had stayed alone while her sister had met someone, fallen in love and had a child. Ophelia never found anyone that she wanted to allow to become close. Many men had tried, none had set her pulse racing. Not like this. Her heart was beating fast, pulse throbbing in her ears. New and strange feelings gave the world an exciting edge. She became aware that she hadn't taken a breath in a while. Helena was staring at her with a quizzical expression on her face.

"That, erm... Well, erm…" Ophelia floundered, uncharacteristically lost for words. "I don't know what…"

Helena leant in, whispering softly into her sister's ear so Tina couldn't hear.

"I think she means she wants to have some adult fun time with you, Ophie."

"I… I… I think I want that too, Hels." Ophie whispered back. Helena couldn't believe it. There had never been any indication.

"Sounds like fun. Ready when you are!" Ophelia said, ignoring her sister's shock.

For the first time since the start of the meeting, a genuine expression appeared on Tina's face. A smile that betrayed a hidden loneliness deep inside.

"Great! Follow me." Tina was already shuffling towards the curtain of water, sensors detected the motion, splitting the flow to allow the two women out.

"Don't wait up for me, sis!" Ophelia said over her shoulder.

"Ophie! Wait!" Helena all but shouted. A hundred questions ran through her mind as her sister turned expectantly. All this time without any indication of interest in romance and she runs off with a woman they barely know? A woman? Was she sure? Why? Is this why she had always rejected men who tried it on? Why hadn't she said anything before?

Realising that it wasn't the time for such questions and to ask them would be churlish at best, Helena sat back and saluted them both with her beer glass.

"Have fun."

Ophelia grinned. The first time Helena had seen her grin that way outside of *Jackie*'s cockpit. Genuine happiness. The two ladies took each other's arms and walked away, disappearing as the water curtain returned. Alone with her thoughts, Helena processed the past few minutes and its surprising revelation. A few moments later, the water curtain split again, admitting the waitress carrying two more beers.

"Your friend's beers." she said matter-of-factly, producing a terminal for payment. Helena checked the balance, frowning as it seemed expensive.

"The sangria is also on there." The waitress' bored tone matched a completely disinterested facial expression. Great, not only had Ms. Drayton run off with her sister, she had run out on the bill as well. Helena paid it without complaint – it was worth it seeing her sister happy for once, not to mention finally getting a contract that would allow them to keep food in their bellies.

Left alone after the bored waitress departed, Helena was left starting at two and a half beers she didn't feel like drinking, contemplating life's sudden twists. They had a way of coming when you last expected them, she thought. Finishing all these beers was probably not the best idea, she thought, raising one to drink. There was still a coolant pump to rebuild and a myriad of other jobs to finish, but she had already paid for them and hated to waste money.

Involuntary Accessory

Adam D. Stones

Rapido Gene Sciences Headquarters, Ganymede, 2272 – Mission Time +00:10 min

Thoughts ran through Marcos' head as he watched the elevator floor indicator slowly tick upwards. Join the Syndicate they said. Earn buckets full of money they said. All tax free and there for the taking. Even a young man of twenty years, without much academic ability could earn more than enough to set him and his family up for life. At least that's what the recruitment agent had told him. For Marcos Salazar, struggling to find work for years, with a two year old boy and another child on the way, there didn't seem to be any other way. The Terran Confederacy paid benefits to the poorest, but it was barely enough to live on and Marcos wanted to provide more for his family. Passing the Jupiter-Saturn Syndicate local office, known as the Jo-Sat Syndicate or just the Syndicate for the sake of brevity, an advert had caught his eye.

"Workers required! Excellent pay! Tax free! Limited time contracts, no running commitment!"

Walking the eight miles home from the job centre through pouring rain, unable to afford even a bus ticket, Marcos had decided it was worth enquiring.

Don't believe the propaganda, they said. It's just the government trying to stop down trodden workers from leaving for a better life, they said. The government wants to exploit you for taxes, we have contracts between equals, they said. Happy workers are productive workers, they said. Free Market competition for workers means thousands of companies based on the moons bidding for your labour. Come to work for a Syndicate company, become trained in the latest manufacturing and development technologies, then if you want to return, you'll be able to earn a high salary as a skilled worker.

It seemed so easy. Home he went, head buzzing with excitement at the promise of future earnings. After discussions with his wife, they agreed to try it for three Earth years. Long enough to earn a respectable sum and train up skills, not so long that the children would grow up not knowing their father. So back he went the next day and signed on the dotted line.

A week later he was on a shiny ship, enjoying a trip to the Jovian temporary dormitory, where his contract with the Syndicate would be bid on by companies needing labour. On arrival he found out the truth. Lies. It was all an enticing web of lies designed to suck in the unsuspecting, the gullible and the desperate. Working conditions in the Syndicate companies were generally terrible. Wages weren't that high, and it had somehow slipped the recruiters' minds to mention how high the cost of living was. All of life's necessities had to be shipped to the various moons, increasing their cost. There was the also the depressing and degenerative effects of constant living in micro-gravity. Muscles wasted away without frequent exercise, vital bodily functions were an embarrassing pain every day involving suction hoses and straps. He was lucky. His contract had been bought by a Callistoan Arms company. At least on Callisto there was some gravity – 0.16g, a fraction of Earth standard, however slight. On some of the smaller moons everyone had to live in zero gravity, which was even more intolerable, but vital for some micro-manufacturing processes.

Conditions in the factories were dangerous, dirty and borderline inhumane. As for training up in skills, he spent his days assembling rifles and machine guns. He was one of twenty workers slotting components together under constant time pressure. It was cheaper and easier to use humans - machines could never quite get the dexterity or range of motion as easily as the human hand and machines broke or jammed, requiring skilled (and therefore expensive) technicians to fix. Cheap labour could just be replaced.

Unions weren't a thing in the hyper-capitalist Syndicate. Marcos had grown up seeing news bulletins of strikers clashing with police in his native Terran Confederacy state of Brazil. He remembered the swinging batons, pepper spray and water cannon. Thinking how unfair it was. Not long after arriving on Callisto, he had seen a video of the one and only strike declared in Syndicate history. The Syndicate Council, the closest thing to a government but which in actuality was mainly responsible for recruiting labourers such as Marcos and settling contract disputes, had found the strikers guilty of *"Breach of Contract"*. The most heinous crime in the Syndicate. So they sent in a handful of Council Enforcers to break the strike.

Labourers with manual tools and a few pieces of power equipment hadn't stood a chance against the augmented Enforcers, sporting the latest muscle replacements and in-built weaponry. Batons and pepper spray didn't seem so bad after witnessing the enforcers using bullets and flamethrowers in what came to be called the Tethys Massacre.

After six months on assembly, Marcos had been moved to Quality Control. Pulling out random weapons and testing to ensure compliance with specification. He had become quite proficient, able to hit the target almost instinctively and it seemed that somebody had noticed.

It was after a couple of months that another company had bought out his contract. It was one of the companies both loathed and adored by the rest of the Syndicate. Specialising in corporate espionage and sabotage, they hired out operatives to steal secrets of competitors for less scrupulous companies. Usually such missions were clandestine, minimal detection-profile affairs since murder and permanent injury were punishable by death. Allowing members to freely kill each other for advantage wasn't conducive to long term stability or profit and the Council punished transgression of this rule severely and quickly. Occasionally, some missions were more active, relying on threat of force to achieve the objective, but if the bluff was called, there wasn't much that could be done. Very rarely, some missions set out with the aim to use active violence. These missions were very expensive and usually a last act of desperation of a failing company, a last gamble to catch up to the competition. If caught, the operatives were subject to summary execution, as were the board of the company ordering the mission. So here he found himself, crowded into a lift with four security operatives and a tech crawler to steal research information.

As the lift approached the control level, another operative shrugged off a holdall and quickly distributed rifles, waiting until the last possible moment in case the elevator camera was monitored. Three fairly standard battle rifles and one strange looking one, a drum magazine under a barrel with what seemed like metallic doughnuts along its length. The weapons distributor claimed that one for himself. Marcos knew better than to ask questions, watching as the man clipped two spare magazines onto his vest. Not that there was time anyway as the lift reached the target floor, gently coming to a stop.

Mission Time +00:12 min

Doors open. Go time. Marcos and three other security operatives launched themselves into the room. The low gravity of Ganymede meant they could rapidly traverse the twenty metre length of the room with ease using low, arcing strides. Panic and surprise spread among the fourteen late shift workers in the company control centre. Marcos had seen it before. These people were scientists, managers and engineers. Violence to them was something that happened to other people or in holo-films, it wasn't a part of their world. Attitude, surprise and rough handling were enough to corral the civilians into a corner. They shouted the clear to their last operative, the tech crawler, still waiting in the elevator. A scrawny woman came out, looking around quickly. Scanning the terminal screens, she picked one to sit at. Marcos had heard of people with cerebral interfaces, but had never seen one. Watching her plug a cable into the back of her neck made him a bit queasy, though it seemed useful. Faint text could be seen in her interface lenses, moving with a speed beyond comprehension. Direct neural interfaces weren't cheap, but allowed extremely fast computer operation especially when combined with the interface lenses which replaced the cornea on the front of the eye.

Mission Time +00:20 min

Too long. Marcos and one of the other operatives were on crowd control, watching the civilian staff to prevent them raising an alarm. Eight minutes had passed and from the expression on the tech crawler's face, she wasn't getting anywhere. She should have been into the system by now and downloading the information. Things were starting to get risky; the initial shock of the incident had worn off but adrenaline was still coursing through the civilians' blood. Some of the braver ones might start to get ideas soon.

Cursing loudly, their tech crawler disconnected and stormed over to Marcos and the civilians, mag shoes thumping against the floor with each angry step.

"They must fucking have some sort of fucking proximity identifier tag on them. I fucking can't get anywhere!!"

She was quite eloquent, Marcos thought dryly. Instead he decided to respond with something less antagonistic.

"What are you talking about? You're supposed to be in the mainframe servers or something by now."

"I fucking know that!" she snapped, "The stupid fucking thing keeps disconnecting. I can't force it to stay open. As far as I can tell from the fucking network traffic, the server keeps looking for a low power signal, some sort of secondary login. When it doesn't see it after a minute, the server disconnects automatically and I have to start right, fucking, over!"

"Can't you spoof it or something?" Marcos asked.

"I tried. I can't. I could confuse you with reasons why, but you're too stupid to understand." She turned contemptuously to the civilians, ignoring Marcos. "Who is going to give me their identifier?"

"We... We... We can't!" a young, small blonde woman stammered, clearly terrified. "If we help you..."

"They're in our wrist bands." A tall, strong looking, fully bearded man stood next to the blonde interrupted, indicating to a rubber strap around his left wrist. He wasn't afraid of making eye contact with Marcos or the other operatives. Marcos mentally tagged him as potential trouble.

"Well, give me your fucking wristband!" the tech crawler snapped.

"I can't take it off. It's connected to the network. It monitors our vitals, as well as allowing network access. If I take it off, it will think I died and raise the alarm. You don't want that do you?"

Smart too, Marcos thought, upgrading his assessment to definite trouble.

"Who can access this console?" the tech crawler asked, indicating her chosen terminal.

"Myself, Greg and Masego." the blonde said, indicating herself, the bearded man and a thin black man standing next to them who, surprisingly, just appeared to be completely bored by the whole thing.

"*Shut up, Stacey!*" the bearded man, apparently called Greg whispered harshly.

The tech crawler lunged forward, grabbing Stacey by the wrist and pulling her out of the huddling group. Mistake, Marcos thought, watching as the situation unfolded, almost in slow motion. Cute, young girl being singled out? Check. Man ready to play the hero? Check. The tech crawler pulled at Stacey's arm, bodily yanking her out. Greg, bearded and brave, tried to free the young woman. Marcos would have put money on the two being romantically involved, or more likely that Greg wanted a romantic relationship but hadn't had the courage to pursue it. Marcos opened his mouth, ready to shout a warning as he started to cycle a round into the chamber of his rifle, intending to use threats and maybe a warning shot or two to intimidate the man into compliance.

Before the warning could even take form, the other security operative slammed the butt of his rifle into Greg's temple, snapping his head sideways. The big man staggered, dazed but not out of the fight. Shaking his head in an attempt to clear the suddenly fuzzy world, the mountain of a man lunged instinctively at the threat, only to be met with an even stronger hit from the stock of the rifle. Striking square on his nose with a loud *crack*, the impact flung Greg's head back as if he'd been clotheslined. Too hard, Marcos thought as the large man stumbled, span a quarter turn and fell backwards in low gravity slow-motion, unconscious head bouncing off the floor.

Mission Time +00:36 min

The plan was falling apart. They should have been on their way to the roof airlock by now, ready for transport pickup. Instead the tech crawler was still trying to gain access to the desired files, while the third security operative held the crying Stacey next to the tech crawler. Stacey was distraught and just kept trying to pull away, shouting Greg's name through tears and sobs, desperate for him to wake up. From her reaction, Marcos changed his opinion to it being more likely they were actually involved. Greg himself was in a bad way. Blood poured freely out of his shattered nose, pooling on the floor by his limp frame. His breathing was becoming ragged and less frequent. Brain damage seemed likely.

Mission Time +00:42min

Greg stopped breathing, followed moments later by his heart ceasing its rhythmic pulsations. Immediately a white light started pulsating in the grey rubber wristband, five seconds later it turned a solid, angry red.

"Oh, *mãe de Deus!*" Marcos muttered under his breath as Stacey collapsed to the ground, with a long wail.

The operation had just gone from bad to a complete shit-show. Every console and screen changed to a lockout, red lights came on as lights extinguished and solid sounding *thunks* came from the elevator doors and other exits from the room. Grievous wounding or killing employees was forbidden. Doing so during a raid was considered "*Hostile takeover by physical means*", another sacrosanct law, never to be broken. He knew that the Rapido Gene Sciences network would have sounded the alarm automatically, alerting Syndicate Enforcers to come and investigate. Without a clear-code from someone in the room, the Enforcers would breach and clear the facility with extreme prejudice. On a moon the size of Ganymede, an enforcer wouldn't be too far away.

Moving away from the civilians, Marcos took a position at the edge of the room, near a support pillar. The other security operatives followed suit, moving to positions around the room. There wasn't much cover – consoles and terminals looked bulky, but a bullet would pass clean through. He watched as the man with the strange doughnut-string rifle took a position in a corner cluster of consoles, with clear view of the elevator. He checked his rifle and cycled a round into his sidearm. It was useless, he knew, they didn't stand a chance against a cybernetically enhanced Enforcer. His only, exceedingly slim, hope was that the other operatives would distract the Enforcers long enough for him to slip out of whatever entryway they came in, giving him time to disappear. That's assuming of course, that he didn't catch the first bullet. Thoughts of his wife and children ran through his head, galvanising him, ready for action.

Mission Time +00:58min

What was taking so long? Enforcers tended to hang around big moons like Ganymede – more companies meant more raids, more contract disputes and more requirement for their response. No sign yet of their arrival made Marcos nervous. The Tech Crawler was plugged into the elevator, trying to create an escape route. Other doors didn't even have power, this was the only exit that responded.

"Any luck?" one of the other operatives asked. He had changed position a few times, seemingly unable to settle.

"Does it fucking look like the elevator is moving?" the Tech Crawler snapped. The floor position indicator still read zero – where the lift had gone to automatically on lockdown.

"Just asking…" nervous operative responded.

The Tech Crawler ignored him, text crawling across her interface lenses.

Mission Time +00:59min

The elevator numbers started moving, increasing slowly.

"Oh, thank God!" nervous operative exclaimed.

"It wasn't me…" the Tech Crawler whispered, a look of horror etched into her features echoed faintly on the other operatives' faces as realisation dawned.

Mission Time +01:04min

Something was bugging Marcos. It all seemed a bit too obvious. The elevator was closing on their floor, numbers approaching their current level. Red LED lights around the sliding door changed to green, announcing the elevator's arrival. Nervous operative shouldered his weapon, chest heaving as the man started to hyper-ventilate. He was already firing as the doors opened. Adrenaline dumped into Marcos' bloodstream, making the world seem a bit slower. He could almost watch the mechanism of the working firearm sliding back and forth, see the sparks from bullet impacts.

Marcos' suspicions were confirmed as the doors opened amid the stream of gunfire, the elevator was empty. His warning shout was lost amid two loud explosions, shaped charges cutting holes in the floor. One was barely six feet away from Marcos. Flying debris arced through the air, before rebounding off whatever it hit and fell at a leisurely pace in the low gravity. Instinctively shielding his face and head, Marcos watched from under his arm as two humanoid figures came flying into the room via the newly made entrances, rotating in the air to land feet first on the ceiling less than half a second later. Enforcers, moving fast. No doubt their responses were accelerated by software and hardware enhancements. The nervous operative was dazed and staggered by the explosions, still firing wildly towards the elevator. The closest Enforcer pointed an arm at the man, allowing a barrel to rise from the forearm of a cybernetic arm. One shot later, directly into the medulla oblongata, nervous operative became nothing but a limp rag doll, Ganymede's weak gravity pulling his flaccid body to the ground in slow motion.

A second stream of gunfire began, aiming directly at the Enforcer which had shot. It might as well have been a water pistol for all the good it did. Bullets flattened themselves against advanced armour composites and titanium alloy enhancements. The second Enforcer fired a shot, as accurately and mercilessly as the first, ending the stream of bullets without fuss. Barely a few seconds had elapsed since the holes had been breached into the room, but half the operatives were terminated. Glancing at the breach hole, he knew it was now or never, time to leave or be unceremoniously extinguished. As he tensed in preparation to move, he saw the enforcers were staring at him, blank helmets pointed in his direction, orientation only given away by the plethora of lasers and sensors around the edge. Two arms raised in his direction, ready to deliver punishment as he closed his eyes. *I'm sorry, meu amor.* He thought, preparing for the end.

Strange sounds made Marcos open his eyes again. High-pitched oscillating humming mixed with a *thwip* sound that he couldn't quite place. The enforcer nearest Marcos had sprouted a large number of thin darts, an equally large number in the ceiling around and behind it. Bodily and hydraulic fluids leaked from holes pierced through armour previously thought impenetrable to anything not vehicle mounted. Jammed by flechettes, actuators juddered and screeched as the enforcer tried to move. Motions became languid as fluids erupting from the wounds slowed, pressure dropping precipitously before a final whine, descending in pitch, emerged from the shattered body as it became deathly still.

"Ha! It works!" came the cry from the man wielding the strange gun.

Enforcer number two pushed off the ceiling, narrowly avoiding a second stream of darts, before flipping over and disappearing behind a bank of consoles. Marcos looked over to see the other remaining security operative, aiming the strange doughnut adorned rifle at the console bank before pulling the trigger and unleashing an insanely large number of darts in under a second. *An electromagnetic flechette gun?* Marcos wondered as he watched the enforcer scuttle out of concealment on all fours like a demented robotic crab, double articulated limbs allowing a disturbing range of motions. Smooth composite body armour panels split apart, creating a gap for a half metre long, quad barrelled cannon to emerge, mounted on a spherical ball mount, a small ammunition belt looped back into the torso opening.

Four barrels span into a blur before a short burst of flame erupted from the barrels, with a corresponding explosion of impact shrapnel from the console and walls near the attacking operative before the barrels stopped as quickly as they started. Marcos decided now was an ideal time to make an exit. The nearest opening was only a few feet away, the enforcer was occupied, not paying attention to him.

As soon as he moved, the cannon twisted in his direction, burping a large number of bullets in his direction. Pain flashed into Marcos' brain as small calibre rounds tore into his side and leg, tumbling and fragmenting on impact to create the maximum wound channel possible, minimising the chance of over-penetration. Muscles ruined, bones shattered, Marcos tumbled to the floor, momentum carrying him several feet in a lazy bounce. The entry hole was excruciatingly close, he could reach out with his free hand and touch it. Scuttling out from behind a console, the enforcer locked onto Marcos, ready to deliver a killing shot…

Flechettes slammed into the Enforcer, peppering the left side of the cybernetic killer. Flailing, the Enforcer fell, tried to stand

and fell again. Barbed shafts were protruding from the legs and arms-become-legs. Only a couple had hit the torso, not penetrating far. Marcos felt a strange pang of pity watching the Enforcer thrash around. It reminded him of a dog he saw hit by a car in his youth – trying to stand but unable to command its limbs properly.

Approaching calmly, the operative was having some difficulty with the apparently complicated process of reloading his flechette gun with a new drum magazine, coming up behind the Enforcer. It hadn't seen the threat, still focussing on attempting to regain control of its wayward limbs. Options quickly ran through Marcos' mind. Try to escape through the hole, leaving the Enforcer and operative to fight it out? Whichever won, the survivor would no doubt be after him, eager to tie up loose ends. Wait to see who won? Chances are neither side would want witnesses. A rifle-sized weapon powerful enough to take out an enforcer with ease would shift political power away from the Council, who wouldn't be enthusiastic about such a thing, or want its existence widely known. Neither would whoever hired them all for this test – at least, he assumed it was a test. The manufacturing standard of the weapon indicated prototype level of production, so they would want it kept quiet until more could be manufactured, with improvements from the field test.

Blood loss started to make him light headed, he had to make a decision quickly. Holding the rifle steady was a challenge, his left arm was sluggish and weak, muscles torn from bullet wounds. Aiming at the Enforcer, he took a breath to steady himself as his target stopped moving, head pointing in his direction, tilted sideways like a dog puzzling over his master's actions. Marcos' vision started to go grey at the edges, his body becoming weaker, colder. Unable to hold his weapon steady, he knew it was now or never. He aimed as best he could and held the trigger until the magazine ran dry.

Mission Time +01:08min

Marcos lay spent on the floor, consciousness a hazy concept. Red light had been replaced with a bright white illumination, which hurt his eyes. He was vaguely aware of someone moving awkwardly around, collecting the flechette gun, pausing only to execute the Tech Crawler cowering under a console – one less loose end. His eyes closed of their own volition.

Mission Time +01:10min

Someone was prodding his shoulder repeatedly. He groaned and tried to roll over. Pain, strangely distant, came from his leg. It should have been more intense, Marcos thought. Instead the sensation was more like listening to a loud rock concert from a distance – you knew the auditory pressure should be overpowering but instead you could only vaguely hear the words. His shoulder was being prodded again, more insistently this time. Couldn't the person see that he was trying to sleep? Some people are so inconsiderate…

Marcos opened his eyes, ready to remonstrate with whoever wouldn't let him sleep. Foul language died in his throat as he saw the Enforcer standing over him, about to poke him again.

"I'm awake. I'm awake, damnit."

"Usually you would be executed without hesitation for your part in this." The Enforcer's voice was metallic and crisp.

Marcos laid back, unsure how to respond. He thought he had been aiming at the enforcer, instead he could see the final security operative slumped against a bullet ridden console, sporting several holes of a calibre that matched Marcos' own rifle. It appeared in his weakened state he had missed his target and hit his fellow operative. The Enforcer helmet opened, segmented sections folding back behind the head. Disappointing, Marcos thought. He had been expecting some sort of cyborg horror show, implants for eyes, cables protruding everywhere. What he actually got was a rather average looking man's face, not too dissimilar to his own. Interface lenses, similar to the ones the Tech Crawler used, sparkled faintly in his eyes.

"What was the purpose of this mission?" the Enforcer asked, staring intently at Marcos.

Marcos paused, normally silence was a part of the contract, but it appeared the people who had paid him had a hidden agenda. Honesty was probably the best policy.

"I was told it was to steal information. I don't know about anything else."

"It wasn't to test this weapon? To see if it could kill an Enforcer?" The Enforcer was still staring at him, Marcos wasn't sure the cyborg had actually blinked during the conversation.

"I didn't know anything about it."

The Enforcer paused, seemingly focussed on the information scrolling on his interface lenses.

"It appears you are telling the truth."

"No shit." Marcos said, as coughing racked his body. He could taste blood in his mouth, not a good sign.

"Having reviewed the security footage, you weren't responsible for the death of the civilian. Nor did you fire on us. Those factors, in addition to the fact you may have just prevented my death, mean I have the authority to offer you a proposal."

Marcos relaxed, blood loss making him sleepy again.

"I'm listening," he said, just before consciousness slipped away.

The Desert Spirit

Mark Ellott

Somewhere on Highway 8, the Sonoran Desert, Arizona.

It was to be the trip of a lifetime. I'd been widowed for a few years and despite several attempts at dating—and don't get me started on the internet dating thing, we'll be here all day—suffice to say, I was still single and carefree. Retirement was looming and I'd cut back my work to three days a week at the most. However, there was one thing I'd always wanted to do, ride from the Atlantic coast of America to the Pacific on a motorcycle. Now, I felt, was the time to do it, before I was too old for such an odyssey.

I'd booked a flight and hired a motorcycle in Washington DC. I'd decided that as I was there, I'd look around the city and set out a few days later. I'd ordered an Indian FTR S. I wanted an American bike but have never really been happy with the cruiser riding position. The FTR was a nice mix of the American style with its big V twin engine and being based on the marque's winning flatracker, had a more European stance when riding.

It did have one disadvantage. As it turned out a big disadvantage, which it seems is inherent in most American motorcycles. It had limited fuel capacity. Ridden in a spirited manner, its range was well under a hundred miles, so I made sure that I took it easy, as once out on the open road fuel stations were sparce enough to be a problem when you only have an 11 litre fuel tank.

I'd made my way west via a winding route, taking in places that piqued my interest. I stopped off in Nashville and on to Memphis Tennessee. Then I headed west to Oklahoma and on to Albuquerque. From Albuquerque, I'd set a route south of Phoenix as I wanted to take in Tucson. Following the road north towards Phoenix, I again rode west leaving Highway 10 and picking up Highway 8 into the Sonoran Desert. That was when I ran into trouble. I'd filled the bike up to the brim, taking my time as you have to let the fuel settle before allowing more to dribble in if you want to get as much into the tiny tank as possible. But even so, it wasn't enough. The bike expired in the middle of nowhere. It sputtered to a stop leaving me stranded in the heat of the desert.

"Bugger."

I took off my helmet and strapped it to the bike. Resigning myself to the inevitable, I sighed heavily and set out on foot. Going back towards Phoenix was a waste of time, as the nearest gas station was over a hundred miles away, so I carried on in the direction I'd been riding, hoping that there would be somewhere I could get help, or maybe someone would stop and give me a lift. As it was, I walked alone and no one came past for hours.

It was hot. The air shimmered above the tarmac of the road, creating a wobbly horizon. Above I could see birds of prey circling. I had no idea what they were. Might have been some sort of eagle or, on taking a second look, vultures. They had huge vee shaped wings and ugly red heads, like something from a science fiction horror movie. Huge great things they were, just gliding round and round, using the air currents to stay aloft. The sky was cloudless and the sun was a burning eye that seared the earth, roasting all below, including me. I took off my jacket and slung it over my shoulder. Sweat ran down my face and into my eyes, making them sore. I tried to blink it away, but more took its place. I wished I had a hat, but as I'd been riding, I only had a motorcycle helmet and that was on the bike—not that it would be much use walking. I had a bottle of water on board and took that with me, but before too long, it was gone. My eyes hurt from the glare and I could feel a headache forming. Breathing was hard in the stifling air.

Nothing came past in either direction. It made me realise just how desolate this place was, how vast the expanse of desert. I thought about the settlers moving west and how they must have felt, travelling mile after mile in this intense heat with no water to be found. You could die out here and no one would notice. I looked up. Apart from the carrion birds. They noticed alright.

Up ahead, I thought I could see someone sitting by the roadside. I frowned. I shook my head. I must have been imagining it, I thought—a mirage created by the heat. I closed my eyes and opened them again, but the figure was still there, a vague silhouette in the shimmering light. Just sitting cross legged looking out across the landscape.

I heard something from behind me and turned. It was a truck. At last! I lifted my hand to wave. It swept past as if I didn't exist, its vortex blowing dust in my face.

"Thanks a bundle."

Oh well, just keep on walking, I suppose.

As I got closer, the shimmering haze gave way and the figure sitting by the roadside became clearer. It was a woman. She was wearing a dark, wide brimmed hat and her hair fell into plaits either side of her face, as was the fashion with native Americans. There was a reservation not so far away to the south, so I figured that a native American wouldn't be such a surprise. She was smoking a long pipe with intricate carvings, that had a small feather dangling from it. Her shirt and pants were dark cotton, and the pants were tucked into worn, dusty leather boots. I could smell the sweet tobacco scent from her pipe as it drifted on the air. Her face was cast in shadow by her hat as she seemed to concentrate on the pipe.

As I got closer, she turned and looked at me. Her face was dusky and had the high cheekbones and dark eyes of a native American, so I figured my original assessment was accurate. She seemed to me to be young. Must have been about thirty, I thought. She lifted a hand in greeting.

"Hello," I said.

"Hi."

"I, er, I ran out of gas," I said.

"Uh huh." She stood with a smooth, snake-like movement and turned. On her left hip was a holster with a pistol—an old style six shooter.

"I er, I was hoping that there might be a gas station nearby."

She smiled and reached to her hat adjusting it slightly on her head.

"Do you know of anywhere nearby I can get some gas?"

She looked up and I followed her gaze. Far above, the carrion birds were circling.

"Turkey vultures," she said. "Some poor critter is goin' to be dinner, I guess."

"I guess. I er, I wondered…"

"Gas station," she said. "Yeah, you said."

"Well…"

She knocked the remains of the tobacco out of the pipe where it drifted into the hot breeze. She rolled the pipe into a tobacco pouch and put it in a pocket. She turned and walked away from the road. Puzzled, I watched.

She stopped and looked back. "You comin' or what, fella?"

"The road goes this way," I said, pointing along the highway.

"Sure it does. But there's a town over yonder ridge. Wanna come?"

"Do I have a choice?"

She shrugged and nodded west along the highway. "You could keep walking that away. It's a long walk, mind."

"Okay," I said. I stepped off the highway, crossed the verge and set out on foot with her. The walking wasn't easy. The ground was uneven and scrubby plants caught my ankles.

I couldn't say how long we walked in that heat. At least heading in a southerly direction, the sun was no longer directly in my eyes, which was a relief. I watched her as she walked, hips swinging easily in a lithe, fluid movement as she sidestepped obstacles, apparently unconcerned about the rough surface. I paused once when I saw something underfoot and reeled a little as I recognised the bleached skeleton of a cow, yet my companion was unmoved by it, walking purposefully past without appearing to notice.

"You native American?" I said.

She half turned without breaking her step. "Half Comanche. My father was Comanche and my mother was white. I didn't know neither of 'em. They died when I was very young."

"Uh, huh. I'm sorry to hear that. You live on the reservation hereabouts?"

She shook her head. "I ain't never lived on no reservation."

We lapsed into silence and I followed her as she walked. She was incredibly fit, I thought, as I struggled to keep up with her brisk pace. She never broke her stride over the uneven surface while I tripped and stumbled over rocks and vegetation.

We reached a small escarpment and as we came to the edge, it dropped away sharply exposing a valley.

"Down there," she said, pointing.

I looked. A small town straight out of the old west ran from east to west along the bed of the valley. One single street. That was it. I was about to speak, but she was moving again, working down the side of the escarpment, with the confident sure footedness of a mountain goat. I scrabbled and slipped as I followed, reaching out to steady myself, breathing heavily as I stumbled. At one point I slipped and caught my knee on a rock.

"Ouch!"

Eventually, we were in the valley, walking to the town.

"There ain't no gas station here," I said.

"Nope."

"Then why are we here? I need gas."

She didn't reply. Instead, she just kept on walking, keeping up that brisk pace as I half walked, half ran to keep up. My legs hurt from the strain and I was gasping for breath.

The town was like an old, abandoned movie set from a spaghetti western. It seemed to me to be familiar. I had that sense of déjà vu you get when you see somewhere you ain't never been before yet feel you have been there, and it sent a shiver down my spine.

"I know this place."

Maybe because I'd seen so many western movies, I figured. I half expected Clint Eastwood to ride into town and start shooting bad guys. Yes, that's why it was so eerily familiar, I reckoned.

Despite that explanation, it was just too familiar. It really did feel as if I'd been here once a long time ago. I stopped in the middle of the street. The background drone of the wind was interrupted by a door banging in one of the abandoned buildings and a tumble weed drifted by, bouncing along the dusty street past the remains of a livery stable. I looked about and took in the sight. I closed my eyes and I could hear the tinkling sound of an off-key piano along with raised voices from the saloon. Laughter and song. I could half see a buggy outside the general store and a young boy loading it with provisions and I could see a lone rider coming in off the plains.

It wasn't Clint Eastwood.

"You," I said.

She nodded as I turned and looked to the south.

"There was a ranch over that way."

She nodded again. "The McAllister place."

"Why do I know all this? Was it part of some movie?"

She shook her head.

"Then…"

Without speaking, she turned and resumed her brisk pace, striding easily along the deserted street. I had no option but to keep following. We made our way along the street, the wind blowing more tumbleweed through the ghost town and I could still hear that door banging somewhere. We climbed a small hillock at the edge of the town. Here we found a cemetery. Once it was lined by a picket fence with a gate. The gate was lying on its side and the picket fence was mostly just a few stakes in the ground, the years of neglect having taken its toll. Scrubby dried weeds grew around the untended graves. She stopped by a grave.

I looked down at the weathered stone marker.

'Sam Langman 1888.'

"Who was he?" I said.

She sighed. "He was like a father to me. Raised me after my family was killed by soldiers. Taught me all I knew. Taught me how to shoot."

I looked across to the town. Still that door banged in the wind. I imagined two duelists standing in the main street each waiting for the moment to draw, knowing that one of them wouldn't be getting out alive.

"How did he die?" I said, knowing the answer.

"Killed in a shootout."

"Who shot him?" I knew the answer to that, too.

"Me."

"Why?"

She looked past me up at the sky. I turned to follow her gaze. The turkey vultures were still circling. Tiny silhouettes against the clear blue backdrop, floating on the thermals. And that door was still banging. Bang! Bang! Bang! I wished it would stop.

"He was dying," she said. "Cancer. He called me out because he knew it would be quick and clean. I had no idea. Not till the doc told me afterwards. Still ain't never forgiven meself for it."

"Surely it was a form of suicide," I said.

"Yeah, but a hell of a burden to put on someone you love, I reckon."

I looked down at the gravestone. '1888.'

"All this was over a hundred and thirty years ago."

"Sure was. Bin a long time."

I looked at her. We had never exchanged names. It hadn't seemed odd, but it should have. "I know who you are."

"'Course you do."

I looked at this woman wearing a dark, wide brimmed hat with a feather in the hatband, her Comanche face and the plaits that fell either side of it, the beads in her shirt and the six-shooter hanging on her left hip. It felt as if we had known each other forever.

"Morning Cloud," I said.

How did I know that? How did I know this place? How did I know about the McAllister Ranch?

"McAllister," I said.

"Yup. Killed my family. I got him in the end."

"I know," I said. "How do I know all this? None of it makes any sense."

I could hear the door banging on its hinges and the low mournful wind droned in my ears, setting my teeth on edge. She just stood there looking at me. None of it made sense. All I wanted was some gas for the bike. I tried to focus on that. This place, it sent icicles down my spine despite the heat. I felt suffocated.

"You aren't real," I said. "None of this is."

She looked up at the sky far away in the direction from which we had come. The vultures were still there.

"Oh, I'm real," she said. "I'm as real as you are, Sam."

Wholly Ghost

Roo B. Doo

Aida Roundtree never expected she'd end up as a ghost, right up until the moment she became one. Not once in her 78 years of life had that possibility ever crossed her mind, but shortly after death she'd been given a choice in the matter: move on to the great beyond or stick around for a while to '*keep an eye on the child*'.

The offer had been made by a slip of a girl, of no real age, who apparently travelled around in an invisible box. She'd arrived at the scene of Aida's death with an entourage, a coterie that included a keep fit instructor of Amazonian proportions, a Chinese, Elvis-obsessed chef and a stunted grim reaper with a dry sense of humour. Aida hadn't expected any of that either, but then again, who would?

Paul Darling was the child in question, the 13 month old reincarnation of Pestilence, one of the Horsemen of the Apocalypse. Aida herself had delivered Paul into the world just the year before, and she had been babysitting him when she passed away. She hadn't meant to fall asleep on duty but the sofa was so very comfortable and Paul had curled himself into her side and was gently snoring. Perhaps Aida caught the *zees* from him; she wondered if sleep was contagious. Certainly Paul's delighted burbles of recognition at the sudden appearance of his long-time comrades, War, Famine and Death suggested to Aida that there was a lot more to Paul Darling than meets the eye. He *would* need watching.

Death had come only for Aida that afternoon, the slip of a girl explained. Finding Pestilence was a bonus, although Aida didn't think the girl seemed all that surprised by the unexpected reunion. Aida didn't quite know what to make of her; she was obviously in charge of the troop of deathcrashers, but really, she was just a slip of a girl of no real age. In a way she reminded Aida of herself when she was young and starting out as a midwife; she had the same look of someone that had found their vocation. Aida liked her, plus the girl had given her a lit cigarette and told her to keep it. Smoking was the one thing Aida immediately missed upon finding herself dead; it was a habit, she knew, but it was one she wore with pride.

Aida puffed on her cigarette as she considered the girl's proposition. She noticed that it didn't burn away and that both it and its ghostly wisps of smoke were now somehow part of her, part of her *being*. She looked at her cooling corpse that was slowly slumping on the sofa, and at the happy gathering going on in front of it. Paul may or may not be Pestilence, Aida was still processing *that* piece of information, but he was still just a baby and, more importantly, still in her care. At least until his mother got home.

She glanced at the watch on her wrist. Like the cigarette and the clothes Aida was wearing when she died, it too had now become part of her also. The watch hands had stopped at five to three, presumably fixed at the moment she died. She had no idea what time it really was nor how long before Jocasta would arrive home. Paul's older sister Molly would be with her and Aida felt a twinge of guilt at the distress and inconvenience she was about to cause the pair of them. And just before Christmas!

Aida made her decision: either she was still asleep and this was one of those fantastical lucid dreams she'd heard about but had never ever experienced, or she really was dead. What was the worst that could happen?

The grim reaper didn't seem happy when the slip of a girl told him Aida was to stay on as a ghost. He warned of 'unintended consequences' and cautioned against 'supernatural meddling', but it was to no avail; the decision had already been made. Aida wondered if the little reaper felt cheated at having to leave empty-handed; although he was very polite and accepted the decision graciously, he had disappeared soon after. Perhaps in a fit of pique or maybe he was on a schedule; Aida wasn't sure about him yet; Death had already indicated that he knew Molly. To Aida's mind getting to the bottom of *that* story was as good a reason as any to take up residence as a ghost in the Darling household. She could keep an eye on *both* the children.

A plan was quickly concocted to lessen the burden on Jocasta and Molly in the short-term. The War woman, called Wanda, was already acquainted with the family, so volunteered to wait outside the flat and intercept their return. She would need a pretext for wanting to speak with Jocasta, but once invited inside, she could take control of the Aida situation. Aida liked Wanda: as well as having the bearing and physique of superhero, she was literally stepping in to save the day; Wanda was every inch a *Wanda Woman.*

It was agreed: the Wanda Woman would wait on the landing outside the flat for Jocasta's return, and the slip of a girl would depart with Chinese Elvis the exact same way that they'd arrived, by invisible box. Before leaving, the slip of a girl – Aida never did catch her name – hugged Paul and whispered in his ear before placing him in his playpen. Chinese Elvis pointed a pistol finger at Aida as he stepped inside the invisible box and disappeared. "Thagyouverramuch."

It was not until later, much later that night, long after Aida's body had been 'discovered' with all the tears and trauma *that* entailed, when everybody had left, been carried out or gone to bed, that Aida stood in the darkened living room alone, smoking and thinking about the enormity of her last day of life and first day as a ghost. She realised that she hadn't thought to ask any pertinent questions about what she could or couldn't do in her new condition, and that information had not been provided. She wasn't even sure when or even if she would see any of her strange visitors again. Would she have to remain as a ghost until Paul's 18th birthday and was no longer a child?

Aida looked at her wristwatch; it still said five to three.

Christmas came and New Year went. Festivities in the Darling household were a little subdued, no doubt due to Aida's sudden death, but on the whole she enjoyed the experience, even if the family weren't aware of her ghostly presence. When she'd been alive and working, Aida would volunteer to work the Christmas shifts; it only seemed fair to allow her colleagues with children to take that time off when she received the gift of delivering Christmas babies. She loved all the babies she'd brought into the world, but the Christmas ones were Aida's favourites. Except for Paul; he'd made an unexpected Halloween entrance, long into Aida's retirement. She'd been gratified to know that she had not only retained the skills she'd acquired over her long career and could use them, but that her mental faculties had not yet departed. Aida was glad of that still.

She spent the first few weeks of ghosthood exploring the parameters of her new existence. The first thing she noticed was that she was actually levitating, even though she was standing. Considering that she could pass straight through matter, including the floor, that made sense. It also meant Aida didn't have to use her legs to propel herself around; she could just will herself to float in any particular direction. Forward, back, left, right, up down; she had complete freedom of movement.

She could even pass through living people, although Aida tried to avoid doing that after Jocasta had walked straight through her. Aida had felt a draining sensation that wasn't exactly pleasant but fortunately didn't linger. Curiously, Jocasta seemed to get an electrostatic shock from the interaction. Aida thought that was very interesting and would have experimented more, but it felt wrong to purposely do so without her friend's consent, and how could Jocasta consent when she didn't know that Aida was there. Aida remained true to her ethics and avoided all unnecessary contact.

Paul knew she was there, of course, but he was far too young to consent to becoming Aida's test subject. He could both see and hear her, and would laugh uproariously when she pulled faces at him. Paul's laugh was purely joyous and highly infectious; even Molly, who was deaf, would join in at her brother's helpless laughing fit. Unlike sleep, Aida already knew that laughter was contagious, a fact born out at Molly's birthday party on New Year's Day. To prevent any accidental 'bodyshock' interactions, Aida watched the proceedings from the safety of the living room ceiling. Paul found this to be hilarious and soon the room full of 10 year olds, dosed up on cupcakes, soda and ice cream were falling about, laughing uproariously.

The only one of Aida's strange death visitors to show up during this time was the Wanda Woman. She popped by and asked loudly if she could use the toilet. Aida wasn't deaf or stupid and knew when she was being signalled to. In the privacy of the bathroom, with the basin tap running to muffle the sound of her voice, the Wanda Woman asked Aida how she was doing and if she'd encountered any problems so far. Aida hadn't but mentioned what happened when Jocasta had walked through her.

"I felt a draining sensation and Jocasta seemed to get an electrostatic shock." Aida explained. "I guess it could have been the carpet."

"Have you tried it anywhere else? Like in the kitchen or the bathroom?" the Wanda Woman whispered.

"No, it's not right to experiment on someone without their consent. Far too much of that has been going on already, if you ask me," Aida opined.

The Wanda Woman promptly thrust her fist through Aida's chest. "I have no such qualms."

There was no static pop but neither did Aida feel the same draining sensation as before. The Wanda Woman hit her again. "Anything?"

Aida removed the cigarette from her lips and looked down at the straight, muscular arm punched through her sternum. "No, nothing."

The Wanda Woman concluded that she might not be such a good test subject seeing as how she was formally the psychopomp for 'WAR' and not entirely human. Aida still thought that the static shock was probably caused by the hallway carpet.

"Have you been outside yet?" the Wanda Woman asked.

Aida was taken aback at the suggestion. The idea of leaving the flat, of going outside, hadn't occurred to her and she didn't know if it was prudent to try. The Wanda Woman explained that it was possible but without the protection of her body, prolonged exposure to the outside elements would eventually cause Aida to erode.

"How long does that take?"

The Wanda Woman didn't know but advised Aida to avoid extreme weather.

Aida wasn't planning on going outside much anyway.

"Only it's your funeral next week." The Wanda Woman said, flushing the toilet. "I dunno if you want to go along. It's forecast to be overcast but dry. Cold, but that doesn't affect you."

Attending her own funeral would be another first for Aida post-mortem, although the Met Office giving an accurate forecast could also be considered a first. "Can I think about it?"

"Sure. I'm here now to see Jo about the arrangements." The Wanda Woman rolled her eyes. "You don't have any family, Aida, and that care home you lived in has been less than helpful."

"I know, it's being turned into a migrant hostel." Aida snorted. "It's strange that I had to die to find a new home."

"No, it wasn't your dying; everybody dies. You were given a choice, Aida. Ghosts are rare. They're the victims of murder or have died in war. Same thing really. I've never heard of soul being given the choice before."

There was a soft rapping at the bathroom door. "Is everything okay in there, Wanda?" Jocasta asked hesitantly.

"Yeah." The Wanda Woman flushed the toilet again. "This needs a double flush. Sorry, I'll be out in a minute."

"Oh, okay." Jocasta sounded embarrassed. "Whenever you're ready. I've made you a cup of tea."

"Thanks!" The Wanda Woman waited a couple of seconds before resuming her conversation. "You remember the short-arse with the scythe?" she asked Aida.

"The little reaper?"

"Yeah, that's Death. He's *really* good at his job but murder victims are a blind spot. He won't acknowledge it, but I've see it happen myself. I mean, the sheer quantity of murder and killing that goes on during war is unfathomably large."

Aida thought the Wanda Woman seemed almost wistful. She wasn't sure she liked her as much as before.

"Sometimes the souls of people that have been murdered can give Death the slip. If they're determined enough."

"Because they seek revenge?" Aida asked.

The Wanda Woman check her appearance in the bathroom mirror. "Yeah, revenge, justice. Some just want to keep fighting but all they can *really* do is watch. They're just voyeurs. Well, you know." She turned off the basin tap. "Look, I've got to get in there. We'll talk again soon," she whispered to Aida and opened the bathroom door.

"Sorry about that, Jo. Dodgy curry from last night." The Wanda Woman's voice trailed down the hallway. "You might want to leave it ten minutes…"

Aida stayed in the bathroom, thinking about what the Wanda Woman had just told her. She most definitely hadn't been murdered, Aida was sure of that. Not that the government hadn't given it the old college try in the last couple of years, what with their Rona lockdowns and their miracle 'cure' that was nothing of the sort. Never before had Aida heard such errant nonsense as that spewed by seemingly serious people about the wondrous Rona vaccine. Babies are born in nine months, not vaccines which require years of safety testing. Aida had refused to take the shot, or any of the subsequent doses, despite the cajoling and threats to comply. As far as she was concerned, the Rona jab was pure poison.

Molly came into the bathroom and closed the door behind her. She started to unbutton her jeans, so Aida decided to leave her to her privacy and join the two women in the front room. She arrived just in time to hear Jocasta say that she was to be cremated.

"Going up in smoke. Not a bad way to go, I suppose," Aida said loudly as she floated past them.

Taken by surprise, the Wanda Woman choked on her tea.

"Are you okay?" Jocasta asked, slapping her friend on the back.

"Wrong 'ole," the Wanda Woman spluttered and croaked between hacking coughs. "I'm okay."

Aida floated up to her spot on the ceiling. *Just a voyeur, my eye,* she thought, sniffly.

The first of many surprises for Aida on the day of her funeral was that, for once, the Met Office had got it right; the day had dawned cold, overcast and dry, just as they forecast. Aida wondered if weathermen give each other high fives for making an accurate prediction. She was half hoping they would get it wrong as usual, and that there would be a raging tornado. She would then have the excuse not to attend her own funeral, but Aida hadn't been a coward in life and she certainly wasn't going to start now that she was dead.

Her second surprise was the transportation that the Wanda Woman had arranged for the family to travel to the crematorium. It was an enormous pink Cadillac, with a white, shiny roof and an abundance of chrome adorning it. The car's white-walled tires straddled the lines designating the disabled parking bay in the forecourt of the flats. The gleaming paintwork and trim of the 1955 Cadillac positively popped against the bleak, urban backdrop of the Elysium estate. Both had been built at the same time; it was an incongruous sight.

"WOW!" Molly cried with delight and skipped toward the car.

Jocasta looked stunned. "Wow."

The Wanda Woman didn't say anything but her amusement at her friends' reactions was evident on her face.

"What are you up to?" Aida was suspicious, but the Wanda Woman simply placed a finger on her smirking lips in response.

The driver was Aida's third surprise of the day.

"Hello, hello," Chinese Elvis greeted Jocasta and Molly and opened the back door for them. "My name is Xi Xi. Please get in."

Chinese Elvis was more soberly dressed than the last time Aida had seen him. He was wearing a smart black suit, white shirt and black, silk tie, with not a rhinestone in sight, although he was still sporting a greasy quiff and sunglasses.

Molly scrambled into the car first, bouncing across the oversized backseat to the far side. She was followed by her mother, who ran her hand over the soft leather, cream upholstery; Jocasta had never parked her behind on anything so sumptuous before. "Just wow."

The Wanda Woman handed Paul to Jocasta. "I'll just be a moment," she said, closing the back door. "Aida, you remember my friend Xi Xi," she said in a low voice. "This is his car and he's going to drive us today. I hope that's okay with you."

"Hello, Mrs Roundtree," Chinese Elvis said amiably. "It's good to see you again."

"Where's the car seat for Paul?" Aida asked brusquely.

Chinese Elvis looked non-plussed.

"She means Pesto," the Wanda Woman told him. "Look, Aida, possibly we got off on the wrong foot last week, but there's nothing sinister going on here. Paul, Pesto, he's family to me and Famine. We just want to spend some time with him too."

"War speaks truth, Mrs Roundtree," Xi Xi said softly. "We care very much for Paul's family. They are now our family and we will help them. Like family."

Aida looked back and forth between War and Famine. "But what about the car seat? It's dangerous to sit him on a lap. What if there's an accident?"

"There won't be." The Wanda Woman opened the car door. "I already checked," she said sliding inside the backseat and closing the door behind her.

Aida looked at Chinese Elvis. "What does that mean?"

"Believe me, Mrs Roundtree, this car is very expensive. I drive it most carefully," Chinese Elvis assured Aida. "You can sit up front with me. I am very happy for you to smoke."

Aida felt a surprising jolt of gratitude even though she knew her ghostly cigarette smoke couldn't actually bother anybody now. "That's something I not heard in a very long time. Thank you."

"You know, smoking suppresses appetite." Chinese Elvis walked round to the driver's side. "For me, cigarettes are the greatest invention ever."

Aida watched him get into the car. Chinese Elvis was right; fatties used to be a rarity back in the days when everyone smoked. Now hardly anyone did and cellulite had gone through the roof. Aida floated herself into the passenger seat of the pink Cadillac, deciding that she rather liked Chinese Elvis.

"Okay," Xi Xi said, looking behind him at the full backseat. "Are we ready to rock and roll?"

Paul shrieked and reached out his chubby arms toward Xi Xi. "Fam. Fam."

"That's right," the Wanda Woman said, lowering Paul's arms. "Time to vamoose."

Xi Xi turned the ignition key and the engine rumbled into life. As the Cadillac pulled forwards, Aida slid backwards. The Wanda Woman yelled in surprise as Aida passed straight through her and out of the back of the car.

Still floating in a sitting position, Aida watched the brake lights go on as the car stopped in front of her. "What on earth?"

Chinese Elvis got out of the car and walked round to the back. He crouched down like he was inspecting the rear tire. "Mrs Roundtree," he hissed, "Did you forget that you are a ghost?"

Aida straighten up. "What happened?"

"The car cannot move you. Only you can move you."

"Oh, I didn't think of that." Aida suddenly felt foolish. "So I need to move at the same speed as the car?"

"Yes. Can you do it?"

Through the back window, Aida could see heads start to crane round to see what the hold up was. She saw the earnest look on crouching Chinese Elvis' face. "I can try."

"Good." Chinese Elvis stood up, smiling. "You just need to concentrate. Hey, you know what's good for concentration?"

Aida float toward the front passenger door. "I dunno. What?"

"Smoking." Chinese Elvis' smile broke wider. "Didn't I say cigarettes are the best invention ever?"

The journey to the crematorium was something of a white knuckled one for Aida, despite the fact that she was unable to grip on to anything, tightly or otherwise. With her cigarette clamped between grim set lips and her palms flat against her thighs, Aida floated in the front passenger seat, peering intently at the road ahead. A couple of times she slipped through the back of her seat when she failed to accelerate in time with the Cadillac, much to the Wanda Woman's annoyance. The only real mishap occurred when Chinese Elvis braked sharply for a late crosser at a zebra crossing, but Aida carried on moving.

She quickly stopped herself and reversed back to the passenger seat. "Whoops."

"You're doing well."

"What was that?" Jocasta asked.

Chinese Elvis realised his error in complimenting Aida. "Oh, you all are doing really well," he told Jocasta through the rear-view mirror. "Such a sad day."

From the backseat, the Wanda Woman rolled her eyes. "Yes, it's an extremely trying time."

And then it happened, just as the high, stone wall that marked the start of the crematorium grounds appeared up ahead, the heavens opened and it began to rain.

For Aida, it was the least surprising thing to happen that day. "Bloody weathermen. Can't they get anything right?"

The Lord's my shepherd; I'll not want.
He makes me down to lie
in pastures green; he leadeth me
the quiet waters by.

Aida stood at the back of the crematorium chapel, listening to the congregation sing, feeling isolated and sad. It wasn't that the turnout for her funeral service was meagre – it wasn't. Aida may not have had any living family but she had made many friends in her life. Apart from the Darlings and the Wanda Woman, residents and staff from Frampton Court, the care home where she'd lived filled the pews. There were former colleagues from her working days, and even one or two she'd helped birth into the world had come to pay their respects. No, Aida's feeling of sadness stemmed from the fact that she had no way of communicating with them. She could try to join in their conversations, share reminiscences and ask how they're doing, but what was the point? In the presence of so many alive, it finally hit home to Aida that she really was dead.

It was a mistake to come, she decided and left the chapel. The pink Cadillac was parked on the far side of the car park and it was still tipping down. She would go back to the car. Chinese Elvis was there and at least Aida could talk to him.

"Sod it!" she said and zoomed off in the direction of the car park. The rain didn't hinder her, the parked hearse that had delivered her body to the crematorium didn't stop her progress, nor did the extensive lawn, slippery and wet, slow her down. Aida zipped straight through the trees and shrubbery that concealed the packed car park, but what she saw next; however, brought her to a stop.

A group of four people had gathered by the Cadillac. They appeared to be admiring it as they moved around the car, pointing out interesting details to each other. Aida could see Chinese Elvis sitting in the driver's seat, looking relaxed and seemingly oblivious of the strangers poking around outside the

Cadillac. He was still wearing his sunglasses and it took Aida a second or two to realise that Chinese Elvis was fast asleep.

She didn't recognise any of people surrounding the car but she doubted they harboured nefarious intentions for the vehicle or Chinese Elvis. For one thing, they all looked underdressed to be wandering outside on a cold, wet January lunchtime. There was an elderly black man wearing paisley pyjamas; a ruddy-faced teenager in a football strip; a purple-haired woman wearing only shorts and a tee-shirt that sported the large, black type number across her chest, and a tall, tanned and handsome man wearing nothing but a bathrobe that barely reached his muscular thighs.

"Excuse me," Aida called to the group. "What are you doing?"

Four heads immediately snapped round in her direction. The four strangers stared at Aida and Aida stared back. They all wore a similar expression of surprise on their faces and, like Aida, none of them appeared to be wet from standing in the rain.

"Hello dear lady," the old, black man called to Aida, stepping forward. "We are just admiring this very fine vehicle. It is not every day you get to see Elvis Presley's pink Cadillac up close."

"It's not the original," the lad in the football kit interjected. "I told you, that's on display in Graceland in America."

"Okay, okay," the old man said with a chuckle. He indicated to his companions. "Do not be frightened, dear lady. This is Craig, Jaki and Simon. My name is Benjamin. What's your name?"

"Aida. Aida Roundtree. You're all ghosts."

"As are you, Aida," Benjamin replied with a smile.

"I know that." Aida floated forward, through parked vehicles and joined the group. "That's my funeral going on back there. What are you doing here?"

Teenage Craig answered with a shrug. "We live here."

"What, at the crematorium? Why?"

"In case any others attend their own funerals like we did. Like you are," purple-haired Jaki replied. "We're building a community."

"Excuse me, Aida," good-looking Simon in a bathrobe interrupted. "Is that a cigarette you're smoking?"

Oh no, Aida thought. *Even after death, I'm going to be told not to smoke. I hope he doesn't tell me it's bad for my health.*

"Yes," she said defiantly and took deep drag. "What of it?"

"How?" Simon shook his head with befuddlement. "I *know* I was vaping when I died but I don't have it with me *now*." He grimaced in frustration. "I distinctly remember. I was having a relaxing vape on my bed after my workout and shower. What if I didn't pick it up and just left it there?"

Aida weighed up whether or not to tell Simon that she'd been gifted the cigarette by the slip of a girl of no real age, but that would take too long to explain. Perhaps for another time. "I don't think so."

Simon looked disappointed but Aida had a sudden inkling; she remembered that on the day of her death, the slip of the girl had *shared* the cigarette with her whilst they chatted. Aida held it out to Simon. "Would you like a drag?"

Simon was hesitant. "Can I?"

Aida shrugged her shoulders. "I dunno. You're the first ghosts I've met."

"Okay." Simon gingerly plucked the cigarette from Aida's fingers. He brought it to his lips and inhaled. "Oh my god," he exhaled rapturously. "Oh yes! That works."

He took another drag and blew out a ghostly plume of smoke that immediately rejoined his body. "Thanks," Simon said and started to pass the cigarette back to Aida "I needed that."

"Keep it," Aida replied. She held up her hand to show him the smoking cigarette she still held between her fingers.

Simon looked from his cigarette to Aida's. "That's fucking awesome!" he cried. "Sorry, I mean that's awesome. Thanks!"

"Whoa. How did you do that?" Craig asked in amazement.

"Aida, dear lady," Benjamin said solicitously. "Could I also trouble you for one of those?"

"Sure." Aida passed him her cigarette and another immediately formed between her fingers.

"Me, too," Jaki said. "Does it hurt to do that?"

"Not at all," Aida said, passing her the cigarette. "And how about you?" she asked Craig. "Are you old enough to smoke?"

Craig gave Aida a look of disbelief. "I'm dead. Who cares how old I am?" He took the cigarette from Aida. "Thanks, being a ghost can be really boring. Hey, you don't have a football as well, do you?"

Aida laughed. "No, sorry, I don't have one of those."

"Shame," Craig said, smoking his first ever cigarette.

The five ghosts stood in the car park, smoking and getting acquainted, unconcerned with the teeming rain that fell right through them. They shared their death stories: like Aida, Benjamin and Simon had died in their sleep. Jaki had collapsed during a breast cancer charity run and couldn't be revived. Craig had suffered a heart attack whilst soccer training. A second one in the ambulance on the way to the hospital had seen him off. All had died in the past two years.

"And none of you encountered the little fella?" Aida asked. Her four new friends looked back at her blankly. "You know, the little reaper. He's about yay high, wears a black robe and carries a scythe. He's a little grim."

The four ghosts shook their heads. "No, nothing like that," Benjamin said. "I came here for my funeral, hoping for closure. The only ghosts I've met are Simon, Jaki and Craig. And now you."

Something wasn't making sense to Aida. The Wanda Woman had specifically told her that ghosts are rare, although common in war, and were a result of being murdered. But none of these people died fighting in a war and they weren't seeking revenge for their untimely demises. In fact they seemed positively sanguine about their deaths and not at all curious as to why they were ghosts at all.

She had to ask: "So, did you all have the Rona jabs?"

The ghosts looked confused by Aida's question, except for Craig who cast his eyes toward the ground.

"Well, I had my two," Benjamin answered. "Why?"

"Don't mind me, I'm just old and nosy. When did you get them?"

"Let me see now." Benjamin looked skyward as he remembered. "That would have been in January and April 2021. I got a whole month's worth of protection out of them before I died." He laughed jovially at the idea but Aida wasn't laughing.

"Oh, I see where you're going," Jaki huffed. "You're one of those anti-vaxxers."

"And you have purple hair but we're both dead," Aida snapped back. "Did you get one or two boosters?"

Benjamin was surprised. "There were booster shots?"

"One." Jaki's nostrils flared with anger. "I got one for the booster campaign November '21, but I died the following July. They're not related. If anything, climate change was the contributing factor in my death. I mean, it was really hot that day."

Aida looked at Simon. He simply held up the index and middle fingers of his right hand, that held his cigarette. "Two, no boosters."

"Craig?" Aida asked gently, turning to the teenager. Craig's head was still bowed but Aida could see his chin wobbling. "I see."

"One," Craig whispered hoarsely. "At school, at the start of September term. The day before I... you know..."

"Oh, Craig, I'm so sorry." Aida wanted to hug the poor boy. He was so young; it was so unfair.

"You wicked, old cow," Jaki threw her cigarette to the floor and stomped on it. "Why are you causing upset? I take it you weren't vaxxed, so why aren't you still alive, Aida?"

"Everybody dies. That's a fact," Aida said kindly. She pointed to the smouldering cigarette that had reappeared again between Jaki's fingers. "A much better question to ask is, why are you a ghost?"

The silence that followed was awkward but blessedly brief. "Because I was murdered," Simon spoke softly.

Craig nodded his head in agreement. "Yeah, I was killed, I know it."

"What?!" Jaki sighed dramatically. "You're not buying this crap, are you? Is it because she gave you a fag?" She turned and threw her cigarette away, but when she turned back, it was dangling from her lips. "Ugh. What is going on?"

"I don't know, Jaki," Benjamin said evenly. "For all of my life, my expectation was that when I die, my ancestors, sorely missed family, the people I loved would welcome me into their warm embrace. There is a reason why I am here and not there. I don't what it is, but I would like to find out. Maybe then I can go home."

Jaki was still not convinced – Aida could tell as much from the look on her face and the tightly crossed arms under her chest. Jaki had a large bosom; it couldn't have been comfortable running with those, for fun or otherwise, Aida decided. And then she noticed the three digit number across her chest.

"Do you believe in coincidence, Jaki?" Aida asked. Benjamin, Simon and Craig all looked at each other.

Jaki shrugged her hunched shoulders. "I don't know what you mean," she answered gruffly.

"Well, do you believe in signs?"

"Like signs from God? Don't tell me you've got one of those as well?" Jaki answered sarcastically.

Aida wasn't phased by the young woman's dismissive demeanour. "See this watch," she said, lifting her wrist. "It's broken. It stopped at the moment I died. I have no idea why I'm still wearing it. I still look at it." Aida shook her head dismissively. "Jaki, what time does it say?"

As Aida held her arm out, Benjamin, Simon and Craig all leaned in to take a look.

Jaki begrudgingly looked at the time on Aida's wristwatch. "It says five to three. So?"

Craig saw it first. "Whoa, no way!"

Simon and Benjamin looked at each other in confusion. "I don't get it," Benjamin said.

"Oh," Simon said with sudden realisation. "It's phonetic. Awesome."

"Ah ha, yes!" Benjamin turned to Jaki. "I see it now."

"See what? It says five to three. That doesn't mean anything," Jaki shouted in frustration.

"Except it's also your running number, Jaki. You're wearing it," Craig explained.

Aida thought Craig had cheered up immensely. He was a sharp lad.

"Jaki," Benjamin said kindly. "Aida's died at five to three. You died *wearing* 523. Can you hear it? It's the same."

Jaki was silently shaking, fists clenched at the end of ramrod arms held straight at her side. It was good-looking Simon, in a far too short a bathrobe to be really decent, Aida thought, who finally triggered her.

"Jaki, sweetheart. Just face it," Simon purred between cigarette puffs. "Aida's got your number."

"ARGH!" Jaki screamed and stomped her foot. It passed silently through the tarmac surface of the car park. "Argh. I'm going. See you later."

Jaki zoomed off in the direction of the crematorium. The remaining ghosts watched her leave.

"Will she be alright?" Aida asked.

"She's upset. She'll be okay once she calms down," Benjamin said reassuringly. "She'll be fi-"

"Oi! Aida!" Jaki called back from the far side of the car park. She pointed toward the chapel. "That's your funeral, yeah?"

Aida nodded. "Yes."

Jaki pulled an ugly face. It was most unbecoming. "Good, I'm going to zap your mourners." She zoomed off.

Now Aida was confused. "What does she mean? What's she going to do?"

"Ah, don't worry, she can't do anything," Craig said. "Not really, except give electrostatic shocks. Man, that's such a weak superpower." He sounded disgusted.

"The bodyshocks are real? That's very interesting." Aida filed that bit of information away for further reflection. Goodness knows she had the time to think about how that might be useful.

"Do you think there are more ghosts at other crematoriums and churches?"

Benjamin took a puff of his cigarette and then placed it behind his ear. "Do you know, Aida, I hadn't thought about that. There could be."

"We could look," Craig added. "I'd be up for some of that. One of them might have a football."

"Are you going to stay with us?" Simon asked Aida. "Don't mind Jaki. She has to learn to be more inclusive. If you're right about the Rona jabs, then we can probably expect our numbers to grow. We could use your help."

Aida was touched by the offer and a little tempted; however, she'd promised the slip of a girl that she would keep watch over Paul, and Aida had no intention of reneging on their deal. Still, it was good being around the other ghosts. They were a nice crowd, Jaki's tantrum notwithstanding and even that was fun. They gave Aida a sense of *being*.

"I'll have to take a rain-check on that, I'm afraid. But I promise you, I'll be back."

"Good evening, everyone!" Simon called from the the front of the chapel. "I can see we have some noobs with us tonight, so I'll just quickly cover some basics first."

Aida sat in the back row of the darkened chapel and looked at the pews filled in front of her. They were nearly as full as on the day of her funeral, just a few short months ago. Simon was right: there *were* a lot of new faces in the crowd tonight, which made Aida feel happy and yet incredibly sad. As usual, all the ghosts in attendance possessed a lit cigarette. Some smoked theirs and others didn't, but all of the ghosts would share their cigarette with any new lost soul encountered. It was a bit like a badge of honour, Aida had decided, except entirely more useful.

She smiled and puffed on the original, the cigarette given to her by the slip of the girl, as she waited for Simon to start. He was becoming quite the motivational speaker, not to mention easy on the eye.

Simon stepped out from behind the lectern and strode up the centre aisle, stopping at the midway point. He waited until he had everyone's attention before starting to speak.

"We're here because we were murdered."

Aida could see heads nodding in agreement.

"You, me, all of us," Simon continued. "Whatever their motives, the authorities we trusted lied to and killed us. They robbed us of both our lives and our natural deaths. There's a reason why we're here. There's a reason why *you're* here."

He looked around at the attentive faces. "Welcome to Fright Club. The first rule of Fright Club is: we don't let them get away with it."

Simon paused dramatically. "The second rule of Fright Club is..."

"WE DO NOT LET THEM GET AWAY WITH IT," the audience roared back.

At the rear of the chapel, unobserved and unperceived by the ghosts attending Fright Club, God and Death stood in her invisible Situation Room and watched the proceedings unfold.

"I did warn at the time that allowing Aida Roundtree to remain as a ghost would have unintended consequences, Ma'am." Death would never gloat, but he did feel vindicated.

Indeed, I remember.

"Do you hear them? They sound very angry."

They were murdered.

"She's building an army," Death continued. "They *are* seeking revenge."

Oh, Big D, an army of avenging ghosts? Surely that's just a little too Tolkienesque, even for you.

"Unintended consequences from supernatural meddling, Ma'am. Aida Roundtree is up to something. I know it."

She's doing a fine job watching over Pesto, according to War and Famine. They have both sent in progress reports. Pesto adores her.

"But do they know about her ghost army?" The conversation wasn't going at all how Death had imagined it would. In fact he was starting to think that God wasn't quite as alarmed at the situation as he was.

I don't think so. I will mention it to War, though. I'm sure she'll be amused.

"Or inspired."

More unintended consequences, Big D?

Death no longer felt any vindication. He remained silent.

The one aspect which I do find most troubling is why weren't these souls collected when they died? Are you looking in to that?

"Unfortunately, a small number of murder victims will go unreaped, each year." Death dropped his head in shame. "However, according to the Aether records, all of these ghosts should still be living people. An investigation is already underway."

You will keep me updated?

"I will, Ma'am."

God smiled down at Death.

Good. Honestly, Big D, an army of ghosts? It's not as if ghosts can do anything...

The Yard Sale

Daniel Royer

Cairo Courier, November 29, 1933
FAMED ARCHAEOLOGIST FOUND DEAD—
GOLDEN CALICO MISSING

Cairo, November 29—A search party yesterday morning discovered the remains of celebrated archaeologist Dr. Cyril Otto. As reported earlier, Dr. Otto had discovered the tomb of King Dod on November 26th, sending an errand boy to relay the news to the Museum of Egyptian Antiquities, of which Dr. Otto had been employed. Dr. Otto never made it back to the museum. A search party ensued the following day, November 27th.

"Doctor Otto find tomb," said the errand boy through a translator. "He find King Dod tomb. He also find Golden Calico."

The object, to which the errand boy referred, is a much-fabled cat-shaped artifact, believed to be hand-carved out of solid gold for King Dod, who reigned over Egypt *circa* 1400 B.C. It is called the Golden Calico, and is considered to be the most important archaeological find since the discovery of King Tut's tomb a decade ago. The priceless artifact is reported to be around 12 inches in height, 5 inches in diameter, with a width of 6 inches, weighing in at approximately 50 pounds. It was carved to the precise likeness of King Dod's beloved cat, a calico named "Cookie Monster."

The search party found the slain body of Dr. Otto in a crevice thirty yards off Pharaoh Road, and three miles out of the Canyon of Crowns, the location of King Dod's tomb. The local medical examiner has ruled the archaeologist's death a homicide, blunt force trauma being the cause of his demise. Not found on his person, it is believed that tomb raiders have stolen the Golden Calico, the theft of which was likely the motive behind Dr. Otto's murder.

Widely considered to be the most influential archaeologist of his time, Dr. Cyril Otto (1894- 1933) had many famed discoveries to his credit: Adam and Eve's apple core, Samson's comb, and King David's slingshot, among many other notable findings. The discovery of the Golden Calico, however, is considered to be Dr. Otto's most substantial achievement.

"Doctor Otto was the greatest archaeologist who ever lived," said the curator for the Museum of Egyptian Antiquities. "If you tossed a needle in a haystack, poured two tons of sand on top of it, and allowed three thousand years of time to pass, Doctor Otto would find that needle. Those scoundrel tomb raiders didn't just rob Doctor Otto and the museum—they robbed the *whole world.* Who knows what discoveries he would have made? Excalibur? Atlantis? The Fountain of Youth? There was nothing he could not find."

The Cairo Police Department is asking the public for any information or description of the tomb raiders, as there is nothing known about them at this point. Additionally, the police have asked all pawn dealers to be on the lookout for any person or persons selling anything shaped like a cat. The Museum of Egyptian Antiquities is offering a one million dollar reward for the retrieval of the Golden Calico, and an additional one million dollars for the capture of the tomb raiders.

Ninety Years Later…

"You'll be selling the stuff in those boxes," said Chuckles, pointing. "Most of it belonged to my great-granddad."

Roger Barton studied the dusty boxes in the corner of the garage. There were about a dozen of them, each one saying GRANDPA. "Did I ever meet him?" he asked.

"No. *I* never even met him. He died when I was a baby. Plus he spent most of his time in Egypt. Mom said he was into some shady dealings over there. That's why she told me to sell his stuff. She wants it out of her garage. It's been a while since she's been through these boxes. Who knows what you'll find in these?" he said, grinning.

Chuckles' mom, Mrs. McGuinn stepped into the garage. She wore a robe and slippers. She smoked a cigarette, surveying the garage. "What you'll find in those boxes is my granddad's old crap," she said, exhaling smoke. "Knowing him, probably a bunch of *illegal* crap. Granddad was known as something of a grifter over there...What are you two clowns doing with it anyway?"

"Mom, you told me to sell it," said Chuckles.

"No. I said to get *rid* of it. It's junk. It's worthless."

"Well, Barton's gonna sell it. He's a professional."

Mrs. McGuinn eyed Barton dubiously. She smoked her cigarette.

Chuckles looked at his watch. "Well, I've gotta head to work now. So Barton, take the boxes out to the front lawn and unpack them. Like I said, I have no idea what's in them, and she probably doesn't either," he said, indicating his mom. "Stay out there all day if you like. Accept cash only. No payment plans. And whatever you make, you can keep half."

"You can count on me," said Roger Barton. He turned to Chuckles' mom. "And don't worry, Mrs. McGuinn. I'm going to make us rich today. Like Chuckles said, I'm a professional."

Mrs. McGuinn sucked the cherry out of her cigarette. She dropped it to the floor, stubbing it out with her slipper. "Big talk," she said.

Chuckles McGuinn was correct that his friend Roger Barton was a professional salesman. In fact, Barton had an array of experience in the sales field, including fire sprinklers, automobiles, timeshares, and even real estate—and all before his thirtieth birthday. It had been a turbulent period in young Barton's life, as he experienced the thrill of almost closing sales, and the heartache of ultimately botching them. It was true that he had faced many challenges in his four years as a salesman. But today, thirty-year-old Roger Barton would be facing his greatest challenge yet: a yard sale.

It was widely known in the industry that a yard sale was the toughest gig in the business. It was easy to get rich selling cars and real estate because that stuff was so expensive. You only had to close on *one* sale to make some serious money. Tragically, Roger Barton had never closed on any of that stuff. That was why he was a grown man living in his parents' basement. Barton's sales buddies said he didn't have the right stuff to be a closer. So did his mother. So did Chuckles' mother. But Barton knew different. Automobiles and real estate were too easy. They were *beneath* Barton. A guy like Barton needed challenges. Anyone could sell cars and houses. But a yard sale was a different story. You had to close on a lot of crap just to break even. Dishware, clothes, toys, outdated technical devices… Most of the stuff spread out in a yard sale had more sentimental worth than monetary value. So, how do you get rich off selling other people's junk? Well, Roger Barton knew a guy that did it, and his name was Barton Senior. That's right… it was Barton's father.

Barton Senior was a legendary salesman in the community. He too had sold cars and real estate. Barton Senior made money. But the old man soon got bored. Cars? Houses? Where was the challenge? Where was the rush? Barton Senior took a gamble and got in the yard sale business. The yard sales got his adrenaline pumping. With yard sales he got his daily fix. The old man closed *hard*. His reputation in the community grew. If you wanted to get rich off the junk in your garage, you better hire Barton Senior. Whatever you had in those dusty boxes up in the rafters, Barton Senior could sell it for big bucks.

Splitting the take fifty-fifty, Barton Senior made himself and all of his neighbors wealthy. Some old lady had a torn-up wedding dress for him to sell. He closed on it for a million bucks when he told a customer that it was worn by some lady named Martha when she married a guy named George Washington. He sold some kid's old magic kit for two million when he said that it had belonged to Harry Houdini. The Barton Family moved into a mansion. They had lobster tail for dinner every night. Barton Senior thought that nothing could stop him.

Barton Senior was wrong. One of his neighbors had some junk for him to sell, including an old baseball bat. Well, Barton Senior sold that baseball bat to some Italian guy for three million dollars when he told him that it had belonged to Babe Ruth. Apparently, the Italian guy was mobbed up, and he broke Barton Senior's legs with that very bat when he found out it didn't belong to the Babe.

Barton Senior was now in a wheelchair. He wore a diaper. He lost the respect of the community. Yard sales were now subcontracted to other salesmen—the closers. The old man could no longer sell anything. He was a disgrace in the neighborhood. The Barton Family had to move out of the mansion. They didn't have lobster tail for dinner anymore. Mrs. Barton Senior got fed up. She made her husband sleep on the couch.

Roger Barton was embarrassed of his father. The old man was pathetic. It turned out, his dad didn't have the right stuff to be a salesman. He was not a closer. Barton Senior now spent his days rolling around the house peeing in his diaper while being changed by local teenagers padding their resumes so they could get into the good colleges.

Roger Barton vowed that he would not end up like his father. Nobody would be changing Roger Barton's diapers but himself. Barton would be a closer. He would prove this to everyone.

But there was someone in particular that he needed to prove this to the most. That's right… it was a girl. She had red hair and worked at the cookie shop in mall. She had pigtails, dimples, and a small cleft in her chin. She was the most beautiful girl Barton had ever seen.

But there was a problem: the redhead wouldn't go out with Barton. In fact, she was downright mean to him. She called him a loser. She said that he wasn't man enough to take her out. It was true that she dated salesmen exclusively, but she only went out with the ones that closed, and that wasn't Barton. He spent most of his evenings nibbling chocolate chunks at the cookie counter trying to woo her. He talked of all the big sales he was about to close. She flirted openly with the other salesmen hanging out at the cookie counter—the ones who closed. The redhead touched their biceps and laughed at their jokes. Most nights she went home with one of them. Most nights Barton cried in his parents' basement.

Roger Barton needed to prove to the cookie girl that he was a real salesman. He needed to close on something *now*. And this yard sale business could be just the thing to take him there.

The redhead pulled a fresh batch of snickerdoodles from the oven. Smells of cinnamon and sugar wafted in the air. She put the tray by the register. As always, a scrum of cocky salesmen were lined up at the counter. They reached for the cookies.

"That's ten bucks a pop," said the redhead. Ten-dollar bills quickly replaced the cookies on the tray. The cookie girl stuffed the cash in her pocket. She loaded up the tray with a batch of shortbreads. She set the timer.

"Like I was saying," said one of the salesmen, nibbling on a snickerdoodle. "I closed on a house last night."

"Well, I closed on a car this morning," said another salesman.

"That's nothing," said a third. "I closed on a yard sale yesterday." The other salesmen began to grumble. He had them beat. The redhead leaned over the counter to stroke his bicep.

As she caressed his arm, a feeling of discontentment trickled through her. She sighed. The cookie girl knew the drill. In a few hours she would be clocking out of work, and this yard sale stud would take her out for a night on the town. And the next day, another sales buck would be doing the same thing. Dating closers was fine, but it was becoming stale bread—like cookies left on the counter too long. Where was the thrill? Where was the rush? Some of her girlfriends often spoke of dating "nice guys." The redhead never really took this practice seriously. It all seemed rather dull. But maybe there was some truth to it? What would it be like to date a closer that was also a "nice guy?" Someone who sold condos in the day, and flew to Africa to help starving folks at night. The mere thought of it got her blood pumping harder. Goose bumps prickled on her skin. The cookie girl was revved up. She removed her arm from the salesman's bicep. She applied a fresh lining of balm to her lips—wild cherry. All the salesmen leaned in, taking in the scent. The redhead addressed them.

"Closing is well and good, but what are you studs doing to help the community?"

A beat. And then: "I'll be working at a soup kitchen," said one man.

"I'll be reading to orphans," said another.

"I'll be changing an old man's diaper," said a third.

"That's hot," said the redhead. She began to stroke his bicep. The other salesmen grumbled.

Suddenly, the phone rang.

The redhead answered: "Cookie store."

"Hi," said the caller. "It's Barton."

"Who?"

"Roger Barton—the salesman."

"Oh, right," said the redhead. "The chocolate chunk guy. What do you want? I'm very busy."

"Wanna go on a date tonight?"

"Look Barton, I've got a bunch of salesmen studs lined up as we speak. I don't need to slum with a dud to get my kicks. These bucks are closers."

"But I'll be a closer soon too," said Barton. "I've got a yard sale lined up today, and I'll be making some big bucks."

The redhead's heart began to beat a little faster. She was getting amped. She suddenly remembered: Nice Guys. She needed to slow it down. "I was just telling these bucks that closing is *okay*, but charity work is where it's at... So... what will you be doing for the community today?"

"I..." Barton said, stumbling. "What?"

"Whose diaper will you be changing tonight?"

"What do you mean?" said Barton.

The redhead hung up. She had no time for nonsense. She turned back to the closer at her counter. She fondled his arm.

"So, stud..." said the redhead. "Tell me all about this diaper..."

Roger Barton felt discouraged after the phone call with the cookie girl. He looked at the boxes spread out on the lawn. He would prove the redhead wrong—her and everyone else. Barton would be a closer by the end of the day. The redhead would belong to him.

Barton staked a sign into the grass: YARD SALE. It was official.

Barton inhaled deeply. He unpacked the first box: a Laptop, a Tea Kettle, a Candle, and a Diamond Ring—an eclectic assortment of listless items, to be sure. Chuckles was right: you never knew what you'd find at a yard sale. Barton began to think. What would his father have done with this stuff? Well, he would have made some big bucks, no doubt about that. Just spin a fanciful tale, and the money would come pouring in. But Barton suddenly remembered what happened to his pops when he tried to grift someone who was mobbed up. The old man botched it, that was for certain—the wheelchair and diaper were a daily reminder. Barton noted his father's error: there were certain people that you did not grift. Tough Guys. It seemed to be the only rule in yard-saling.

A car pulled to the curb. A husband and wife got out. The man wore a tweed jacket with elbow patches. The woman lit his pipe. Barton thought the man looked like a librarian—not a tough guy at all. Barton picked up the laptop, holding it like a game show host.

"What you got there?" asked the woman.

"What I've got is a laptop," said Barton.

"We're not interested," replied the man.

Barton thought quickly. "Are you interested in *Huckleberry Finn*?"

"Um... the book?" he asked.

"That's right," said Barton. "Hemingway happened to write that book on this laptop. I'll let you have it for a million bucks."

The couple stared. Barton stared back. The pipe fell out of the man's mouth. He began to say something. Nothing came out. His wife patted his shoulder.

Barton knew he was on the verge of a sale. He put a cherry on top: "It was F. Scott Hemingway's favorite computer. He traded it for a pack of smokes during the Civil War."

The man clutched his heart suddenly. He dropped to the grass. His wife tended to him.

"Is he all right, miss?" asked Barton.

"He'll be fine, young man," she replied. "He's an English professor. I'm sure it's just a stroke."

After the ambulance left, Barton reviewed the scene that had just taken place. *Where had he gone wrong?* Barton did a computer search on his phone. He realized that he had been incorrect on a few details. Rookie mistake. This, Barton realized, was the second rule in yard-saling: Get Your Facts Right. Barton picked up the tea kettle, and studied it. He pressed a few buttons in his phone. Barton got his story straight.

A woman approached.

"Hi ho," said Barton. "Can I interest you in this tea kettle?"

"Tell me more," said the woman.

"What I can tell you, is that Abigail Adams served tea with this very kettle during the first Continental Congress. John Hancock burned his tongue when he sipped too fast," he added, chuckling. "I can let you have it for a million bucks."

The woman wrote Barton a check, and walked away with her tea kettle. Barton stuffed the check in his pocket. A nerd approached.

Barton held the candle.

"Is that a candle?" asked the nerd.

"Sure is," said Barton. "It belonged to Marilyn Monroe. Ever heard 'Candle in the Wind?'"

"The Elton John song?" asked the nerd.

"That's right," said Barton. "This is the candle in the song. It's worth two million, but I'll let you have it for only one."

"That's half off!" exclaimed the nerd. He withdrew a checkbook and pen from his pocket-protector. "Who do I make the check out to?"

"Make it out to 'Roger Barton.' And that's 'Barton' with a 'B.'"

The nerd handed over his check.

Barton picked up the diamond ring, the final item in the first box. He concocted a story.

A man approached. He had a mohawk and wore a wife-beater tank top. Tattoos covered his face and neck. Thick muscles bulged from his arms. His veins pulsed as he walked. Barton could see that he was carrying a gun. Barton got the shakes.

"Yo," said Mohawk. "What's up with that ring?"

"Not much," said Barton, remembering what happened to his father. "It's just a plain old ring. The diamond's not even real. In fact, this particular item is not for sale."

Mohawk walked away, twirling his gun. An old woman approached.

"What's the story behind the ring?" she asked.

"Well," said Barton, "it's about a hundred carats, and you'll never guess who it belonged to..."

It was late afternoon, and Barton's pockets were stuffed with checks. There was one box left, still unopened. Barton had sold the contents of all the others. He was a closer! He thought of his old man rolling around in a wheelchair wearing a diaper. Pathetic. Barton thought of the sweet redhead at the cookie store. He knew that she only dated closers. *Well, babe, guess who joined the club?* Tonight, surely, he would be taking her out for a night on the town. He paused mid-thought, remembering their conversation on the phone. What was all that talk about good deeds and diapers? Barton needed to figure that out.

He was about to open the last box, when Mrs. McGuinn walked out on the lawn. She studied Barton, smoking at him.

"Where's all my crap?"

"I sold it, Mrs. McGuinn. My pockets are filled with checks. I'm a closer. I'm going to take a redhead out on a date."

Mrs. McGuinn blew smoke. "I remember when a girl had standards."

"But this one does, Mrs. McGuinn. She only dates closers... *and* nice guys that change diapers… That's me!"

Mrs. McGuinn stared at him, deadpan. "You're sick, Barton." She flicked her cigarette and went back in the house.

Barton turned his attention to the box. He opened it. There was some sort of sculpture inside. Barton picked it up. The sculpture was gold and shaped like a cat. It was heavy, maybe fifty pounds or so. Barton put it down. At the bottom of the box was an old cutout news article.

Cairo Courier, November 29, 1933
**FAMED ARCHAEOLOGIST FOUND DEAD—
GOLDEN CALICO MISSING**

Barton read the newspaper clipping. When he finished, he read it again. His heart pounded. *The priceless artifact is reported to be around 12 inches in height, 5 inches in diameter, with a width of 6 inches, weighing in at approximately 50 pounds. It was carved to the precise likeness of King Dod's beloved cat, a calico named "Cookie Monster."* Barton checked the dimensions of the sculpture. Holy smokes, they matched! Roger Barton was in possession of the Golden Calico! He had heard of the artifact, of course. Every grade-school kid knew the story of poor Dr. Otto and the despicable tomb raiders who had robbed him. But how did the sculpture get in this box? Barton thought back to his conversation with Chuckles about his great-grandfather: *He spent most of his time in Egypt. Mom said he was into some shady dealings over there.*

Barton couldn't believe it! Chuckles' great-grandpa was a tomb raider! He had murdered Dr. Otto, stolen the Golden Calico, and now that priceless artifact belonged to... Roger Barton. Well, half of it belonged to Barton. The other half belonged to Chuckles. He and Chuckles were going to be rich! But how rich? Barton scanned the bottom of the article once more. *The Museum of Egyptian Antiquities is offering a one million dollar reward for the retrieval of the Golden Calico.* A million bucks! But Barton had heard of a little thing called "inflation." He knew that a million bucks back in 1933 would be worth a whole lot more now. He pressed a few buttons in his phone. Why, that money would be worth over twenty-three million dollars today!

Roger Barton was now wealthy almost beyond measure. He would buy a yacht, and he and the redhead would sail around the world. Barton thought of all the salesmen hanging around the cookie counter. *Tough luck, fellows. There's a new closer in town!* Barton thought of his mom, and Chuckles' mom, and all the people that didn't believe in him. He thought of his old man getting his diaper changed by strangers. *Take THAT, Dad!*

Suddenly a black car pulled up in front of the house. The driver got out and opened the back door. A tall olive-skinned man with silver-slicked hair stepped out. He wore a sleek silk suit. The old man held out his hand and the driver kissed his ring. The olive-skinned man approached Barton.

"*Ciao*," said the man. "My name is Don Carmine Caruso. I look for bargains."

"Well, I've got them…" said Roger Barton. "The name's Barton." They shook hands.

"What do you have for sale, *Signore* Barton?" asked Don Caruso.

Barton reached into the box, pulling out the Golden Calico. He held it proudly.

"*Santa Maria!*" exclaimed the Don. "What is that you are holding?"

This man seemed tough, albeit in a different way than Mohawk. Roger Barton thought back to his father's incident with a tough guy. But Barton then realized he had no need to fear. The first rule of yard-saling did not apply, because the second rule of yard-saling was already confirmed.

"What I'm holding is a little something called the 'Golden Calico.' Ever hear of it, pops?"

"*Si*," said Don Caruso, his eyes twinkling. "*D'oro gatto...*" he said quietly. "*Quanto?*" he asked.

Barton pointed to the bottom of the news article. The old man studied it. Barton spoke: "The Museum of Egyptian Antiquities is willing to pay over twenty-three million for this piece, but I'd be willing to let you have it for an even twenty-two."

"*Molto generoso!*" exclaimed Don Caruso. He whistled over to the chauffeur. "*Ventidue milioni!*" he shouted over to him. The driver opened the trunk of the car. He took out a briefcase, and carried it over to the Don. He opened it for the old man to see. Don Caruso nodded to him.

The Don took the briefcase, and handed it over to Barton. "Twenty-two million," he said.

Barton opened the briefcase. It was stuffed with hundred dollar bills—more hundred dollar bills than Barton thought existed. He closed it quickly. He handed Don Caruso the Golden Calico. The old man handled it, feeling its heft. He smiled, passing the antique over to his chauffeur.

"You are a good young man," said Don Caruso, pinching Barton's cheek. "Back in the old country, you're what my people call, a *venditore*—a closer… May I ask if you are a single man, *Signore* Barton? You have my blessing to take the hand of my granddaughter, my *nipotina*. Take my word, she is very *paffuta*—what you call, 'curvy.'"

"No thanks, pops," said Barton. "There is a girl I've already got my eye on. She is what your people call, *bellissima*."

The Don grinned. "Oh *si*," he said. "I know of what you speak, *Signore* Barton. This is what we call '*amore*.' I am no stranger to this condition, as I myself have a heart that beats for a *speciale* lady—a *bella donna*. This beautiful woman drives me *pozzo!* But I am advanced in years, and I fear that she will not take my hand… But that is not a concern to a young strong bull like yourself... Ah... but to be a young man again, like you *Signore* Barton... I bet you can take your pick of the ladies."

"I do all right."

"*Bravo*," said the Don. "And now I must leave. *Gracie, Signore* Barton." He extended his hand to Barton, the palm facing down. Barton kissed his ring.

Don Caruso shuffled away. "Enjoy your cat," said Barton. He watched the chauffeur open the door for Don Caruso. The old man nodded to Barton once more. The chauffeur got in the car and drove away.

Barton was elated. He dialed the number to the cookie shop.

"Cookie store," answered the redhead.

"I'm a closer," said Barton.

"Who is this?"

"It's Barton. I just sold the Golden Calico for a sweet twenty-two million."

The redhead whistled. "That's some hot stuff, stud. What you gonna do with all that bread?" Barton could hear her applying balm to her lips—wild cherry if his guess was right. He could practically smell it through his phone.

"I'm gonna buy some chocolate chunks—a dozen of them. Maybe even a *baker's* dozen. And then I'm gonna take a beautiful redhead for a night out on the town. Dinner, dancing... the works!"

The cookie girl purred. "But what about charitable works?" she asked. "Closing big deals is pretty boss, but I only date bucks that also—"

"I'm gonna change an old guy's diaper first," blurted Barton.

"You're revving my engine, stud. That seals the deal. Pick me up at eight."

Barton hung up. He was ecstatic. After all these years, he had finally won the heart of the beautiful cookie girl. He sat down on the lawn and opened up the briefcase. He began to count the money.

"Where did you get that dough?"

Barton turned. Standing above him was Mrs. McGuinn, still smoking, still in her bathrobe.

"This came from a little something called the 'Golden Calico.' I got a cool twenty-two million for it."

"Someone paid twenty-two million for that piece of junk?"

"It's not junk, Mrs. McGuinn. It's authentic. I'm not sure if you're aware, but your granddad was a tomb raider. He stole this from a famous archaeologist after he killed him."

Mrs. McGuinn choked on smoke. She pounded her chest and laughed outright. "Grandpa wasn't a tomb raider! And that hunk of crap sure ain't the Golden Calico."

"But... but... but... you and Chuckles said he was in Egypt. Y-you said he was a grifter..."

"He sure as hell was a grifter, but he wasn't no tomb raider, I can tell you that. The old man was a conman—a charlatan. He didn't have the finesse or the guts to be a tomb raider. He sold knockoff trinkets—forgeries. Like those fake Oscar statues they sell on Hollywood Boulevard. You didn't think that stuff was real, did you?"

"Of c-course not," stammered Barton. His brain was exploding. "So… are you saying that that wasn't the *real* Golden Calico…?"

Mrs. McGuinn scoffed, exhaled smoke. "Maybe you *are* a closer, Barton. You just sold some worthless garbage for a hell of a lot of money."

Barton was frantic. Yes, he had indeed sold some worthless garbage for a ton of money… to a man who was clearly a mobster! He had broken *both* rules of yard-saling.

And that was when Roger Barton was grabbed from behind by a pair of very strong arms. He was thrown to the ground. Standing above him was Don Caruso. The old man stood tall, shaking with rage. In his hands he held the 'Golden Calico.'

"How dare you sell me this forgery—this *il falso!*" The old man chucked the statue violently to the grass. Mrs. McGuinn began to laugh. She sat down on the porch and lit a cigarette. Don Caruso continued: "My antique scout says that this is a counterfeit, a fake! Like those junk statues they sell in Los Angeles... I thought you were a closer, *Signore* Barton—a *venditore!* Imagine how my granddaughter will feel when she finds out you are a grifter, a loser!"

Roger Barton began to sob. "He cries like a woman," Don Caruso said to the chauffeur. "Take him away." The driver dragged Barton over to the black car. He popped the trunk. The chauffeur grabbed Barton's upper body, but struggled to get him in the trunk. Mrs. McGuinn, still laughing, flicked her cigarette, and walked over. She grabbed Barton's legs, assisting the chauffeur. The driver closed the trunk once Barton was inside.

Don Caruso turned to Mrs. McGuinn. "*Gracie, signora.* You are a good woman. May I ask if you are single? My son is unattached, and you have my blessing to take his hand in marriage… Also, may I bum a smoke?"

Roger Barton awoke in a windowless room with a tarp on the floor. He was tied to a chair.

"He finally awakes," said Don Caruso to his chauffeur. The Don stubbed his cigarette on a wall. The driver handed him a baseball bat. The Don turned to Barton. "Now *Signore* Barton," he said, striking the bat softly against his palm, "what do you have to say for yourself before I conduct this business—this *gli affari?*"

"I don't have anything to say, Don Caruso," said Barton, crying. "I tried to be a salesman, I tried to be a closer. But I'm not. I'm just a loser like my old man. He got his legs broken by a wiseguy when he tried to con him. Now he's in a wheelchair. He wears a diaper. And so will I. It's no wonder that this beautiful woman won't go out with me."

Don Caruso slumped his shoulders. He put down the bat. "You have just said many things, *Signore* Barton. You are not the first man I have held captive in this windowless room with a tarp on the floor. There have been others that have come before you. It was many years ago that a man tried to sell me a baseball bat. It was this very bat that I am holding now. This man, he told me it had belonged to a baseball player, your American slugger Babe Ruth. But this bat did not come from your Babe, and the man who tried to con me was your father, your *padre*. I put your *papa* in a wheelchair and I put him in a diaper, just like many others afterwards. But you see I am an old man now. I have a forgiveness in my heart that I did not have when I was a young man—a *giovanotto*. I now have compassion for young men like yourself. I have a certain, shall we say empathy for a youngster like you, who yearns for the hand of a *bella donna,* as I, an old man, yearn myself. It may be over for me, over for your father, and over for many others who once sat in this room, but it does not have to be over for you. Therefore, *Signore* Barton, I offer you... *perdono...* Release him from his straps," he said to the chauffeur.

The driver untied Barton from the chair. Barton remained seated. He wiggled his arms, feeling his blood begin to flow again.

"Thank you, Don Caruso! Thank you!"

"There is one favor, *Signore* Barton, that I hope you will grant me..."

"Anything!" said Barton.

"You are very kind. As I have mentioned, there is a *bella donna* for whom I yearn. So far, she has refused my hand, but perhaps you can help me. I am afraid this will be my final chance... You can be, how you say, my man with the wings."

"'Wing-man,'" corrected Barton. "I'd be happy to help in any way I can, Don Caruso. What can I do for you?"

The Don nodded to his chauffeur. The driver opened a closet door. Inside, sat a wheelchair, and on top of the wheelchair rested an adult diaper.

"*Signore* Barton. There is a young woman with hair that is, how you say, *rossa*—as red as the sun that rises. She works in the cookie store at the mall. This *signora,* as I am told, only dates closers. Now, I myself am a closer, a *venditore.* But it seems the young lady has added a new mandate to her repertoire: Nice Guys. Men who do good things for others. Charity—*beneficenza.* I admit that I do not have much experience with this, but I am told that the changing of diapers is of particular significance to this *rossa.* So... my driver will take you and I to the shopping mall. I will push you around in this wheelchair, and when we are in view of this *bella donna,* I will change your diaper. Your debt will be repaid, and the hand of this cookie girl will belong to me."

Barton squirmed in his seat. "Um, with all respect, Don Caruso, I'm afraid I must refuse..."

The Don sighed. "I apologize *Signor Barton.* It seems my English has failed to express my yearning for this fair lady..."

"Oh no, sir," said Barton. "Your English is fine. I understand your yearning, and I sympathize with you very much. I just can't wear that diaper."

The chauffeur picked up the bat. He approached Barton, speaking for the first time. "Never mind me, Barton... Who I am, and what I do for Don Caruso isn't your concern... Except to say that I have worked with the Don for a long time, and have stood by his side in this windowless room with a tarp on the floor more times than I can count. I met the Don when he first arrived in this country many years ago—long before he drove around with million dollar briefcases, I can tell you *that*. I'll spare you the details of what happened between then and now, but suffice to say, the Don did not speak a drop of English when he got off that boat. One of my many duties over the years—including those which go on in this windowless room—is to act as the Don's *translator*. But, since Don Caruso is an intelligent and motivated man, he speaks very well now, and my duties as translator have been limited as of late..." The chauffeur began to palm the bat. "But English is a complex language. A stranger to this land cannot be expected to speak as fluidly as its native sons, like you or me. And so I find that I *still* have to act as translator for the Don from time to time. And, as his translator, it is my belief Barton, that you and the Don had a miscommunication a minute ago. I believe that his English—as proficient as it is—failed to demonstrate the deep yearning he has for this lady. Additionally, I believe that it failed to convey the extent of the debt of which you owe, which, might I add, is considerable… So..." he said, standing tall before Barton, the bat knocking his palm, "was there a miscommunication, or was there not?"

Barton shook in his chair. He thought of the cookie girl. He thought of his dad. He thought of the bat. He spoke, turning to the Don. "I beg your pardon, Don Caruso, but your chauffeur is right. I didn't fully appreciate the scope of your yearning. But now I do... So, of course I will do this favor for you."

"*Gracie,*" said Don Caruso, bowing his head. The chauffeur stepped aside, relinquishing the bat. The Don held out his ring to Barton. Barton thought of the cookie girl once more, and kissed it. "*Bravo!*" exclaimed the Don. He checked his watch. "We must go quickly, *Signore* Barton. This cookie shop closes at eight."

The chauffeur picked up the diaper. He stretched it out for Don Caruso to see.

The Don nodded. "As I think you will find, *Signore* Barton, it is a perfect fit."

The redhead took the final tray of cookies from the oven. She placed it on the counter. Oatmeal raisin steam poured outwards. The salesmen at the counter grabbed greedily.

"Twenty bucks a pop," said the redhead. Twenty-dollar bills fluttered towards the register.

The redhead checked her watch. 7:30. The yard sale stud Roger Barton would be picking her up in thirty minutes. The prospect of dating a nice-guy-closer was thrilling, but she couldn't help but be a little wary of another cocky young buck, even if he fit her criteria. The cookie girl realized that it was easy to *say* that you're a "nice guy." These were *salesman* after all—brash cocky hustlers who talked a big game to close the deal. But who really knew if they were feeding the blind and clothing the poor? The redhead certainly hadn't *seen* them doing this. If she had learned anything in her dating life, it was that brash young hotheads were willing to say just about anything to take her out. Young bucks, she had realized, lacked the temperament of the older studs. In fact, the cookie girl had begun to notice that some of her girlfriends were starting to date older guys these days. Men with mileage. Men with culture and substance and more complications than that of their younger counterparts. Men with baggage were more of a challenge. Yes, thought the redhead, nice older guys were definitely where it was at—as long as they closed, of course.

And it was at that moment that she saw an aged Italian gentleman wheeling a young guy in a chair. The old man was finely tanned with a sharp silvery lion's mane. He wore a slick three-piece suit that complimented his features handsomely. This Italian was clearly a closer. The cookie girl watched him.

The old man wheeled the chair closer to the cookie counter, but stopped abruptly, just a few yards short. He pulled out a knapsack and withdrew a white object. He turned over the young man, and began to change his diaper. The cookie girl swooned.

The aged man sprinkled baby powder when he was finished. He turned to the cookie counter for the first time. He locked eyes with the redhead. The little hairs on her arms buzzed. He smiled at her. She smiled back. The redhead applied wild cherry balm to her lips.

Leaving the wheelchair where it was, the older man approached the counter, his ring reflecting the neon light of the cookie sign.

Gulp, Spit

Daniel Royer

The runner could see the 15-Mile marker in the distance—behind the marker, an aid station with volunteers serving cups of water and sports drinks. This was a marathon—eleven-plus miles to go. The runner was first in the pack. An eager volunteer emerged from the refreshment table, meeting the runner on the side of the road, his gloved hand extended, offering a paper cup filled with a blue sports drink. The runner reached for the cup, grabbing it—not a drop spilled in the exchange. The runner tilted the cup to his lips. Sweet sugary electrolytes filled his mouth. He sloshed it around his tongue, letting it coat his gums as he ran. The runner slid a little down his throat and spat the rest out.

Gulp, spit.

He repeated the process, chucking aside the remainder of the drink, crushing and tossing the cup to the side of the road.

Fifteen miles down, just a little over eleven to go.

The runner's wife and his sister waited with the spectators at the finish line. Their man was an elite runner—he was expected to finish the marathon first or second.

There's a runner coming, someone shouted. The wife and the sister looked down the course. Indeed, a runner was coming in.

It was not their man.

Nor was the next runner. Or the next. Or the one after that.

Ten, twenty, thirty minutes passed. Their runner should have finished by now.

That's when the wife's phone began to ring.

The doctor checked on his patient: coma—suffered cardiac arrest on a race course two hours prior. He had collapsed near the 25-Mile marker, only one away from the finish line. The patient's wife and sister were outside in the waiting room. The doctor did not like the man's symptoms. Sure, runners suffered heart-attacks during the course of a race... it was rare, but it happened. But the doctor had checked the man's medical history. Thirty years old, experienced runner, and his health was pristine. This one didn't feel right. That's why he ordered the blood tests.

The blood test results were now in his hands. Traces of Brodifacoum found. In other words: Rat Poison.

The doctor picked up the phone.

"The paramedic report states he collapsed just short of the twenty-five mile marker," said the doctor to the two detectives in the hallway. One was tall, fifty-five, single: Detective Oslo. The other stocky, thirty-four, married: Detective Gringer. Oslo took notes, both listened. "He arrived about eight hours ago. His condition is critical." The doctor reviewed his notes. "Chuck Broom. Thirty years old. Experienced runner. He's an elite—that means he gets money and sponsorships. His wife—she's in the room with him—she says he travels all over doing these races."

"How long is a marathon?" asked Gringer, the stocky one.

"Twenty-six miles," said the doctor. "Twenty-six *point* two," he added.

"Because twenty-six isn't enough," chuckled Gringer. "What kind of sadist would run that far?"

"'Masochist,'" corrected Detective Oslo. "And one that cares about his next birthday." Gringer shrugged, lit a cigarette.

"There's no smoking in here," said the doctor. Gringer shrugged, flicked the cigarette.

Oslo turned back to the physician. "Continue, Doctor..."

"The paramedics gave him the paddles—that's when he fell into a coma. He was unconscious by the time he got to me. His symptoms felt wrong, so I ordered some tests. We found massive quantities of Brodifacoum in his system. Rat poison. It was ingested. In other words, detectives, Mr. Broom was poisoned."

The detectives let that hang there a minute.

"Is he going to make it, Doc?" asked Gringer.

The doctor sighed. "I really don't know—in fact, at this point..." He didn't finish.

"Tell me, Doctor," said Oslo, "How long does it take for Broadifa—er, rat poison to take effect?"

"Normally it could take several hours, or even days. But this was a particularly significant amount. Add to that, the process would have been sped up because he was running—his heart would have been pumping that stuff through his system like crazy. I'd say, under those conditions, thirty minutes to an hour."

"How long's it take someone to run a marathon, Doc?" asked Gringer.

"That depends of course. Three to five hours for the average man. But with an elite like Broom, probably a click north of two hours."

Oslo put his pencil down. He looked up. "He was poisoned during the race."

The doctor nodded.

Oslo thought about it. "Could it have been spiked in a drink?"

"Most certainly," said the doctor.

Oslo checked the witness reports. He and Gringer had interviewed dozens of spectators earlier in the morning. Broom had collapsed at roughly 1:55:00 on the time clock. Oslo did the math: thirty minutes to an hour would mean Broom had been poisoned somewhere between 55:00– 1:25:00 on the clock. It had happened at one of those aid stations—the ones where volunteers pass out the cups of water and juice. Oslo knew there could be over a dozen during the course of a marathon. He and Gringer needed to narrow that number down to figure a kill-zone.

"And *that's* why I'm not a runner," chuckled Gringer.

"You're not a runner because you're fat," said Oslo.

"Being a runner is what saved Mr. Broom's life," said the doctor.

"How so?" asked Gringer.

"Gulp, spit..." replied the doctor. "My wife's a runner. You see, detectives, those little cups of water and juice that they give out at the races... the runners don't just *drink* them. They put a little in their mouths, wash it around, swallow a little, spit the rest out. Gulp, spit... If Chuck Broom had drank that whole cup, my guess is he would have been dead long before the ambulance arrived."

Shortly after, Oslo and Gringer interviewed the wife, Kathy Broom. The victim's sister Sarah was present as well. They were in the intensive care unit with Chuck Broom. He lay unconscious in bed. Tubes snaked in and out of his body. A respirator breathed for him. A computer monitor beeped. The wife and sister sat by his side. Oslo and Gringer stood above them.

"He travels the country doing these races," said the wife Kathy, dabbing her eyes. "He's placed in Boston and New York. This has always been Chuck's favorite race though—it's a local one—we live in town. He and Stacks have a friendly rivalry—they usually come in first or second. Stacks is local too."

"Who is Stacks?" asked Oslo.

"Stacks Miller—he's the man that won today," said Kathy.

"Stacks is a childhood friend," added Sarah, the sister. "Chuck and I have known him since we were kids. He's an elite as well."

"Chuck was leading the pack when he collapsed," said Gringer, to no one in particular.

Kathy and Sarah said nothing.

"Mrs. Broom," said Oslo. "Perhaps you can help us with our timeline. We know that your husband was poisoned between fifty-five minutes to an hour twenty-five on the time clock. It would give us a better idea of who and where this happened if we knew Chuck's pace… Tell me, what is his mile-time?"

"Five minutes," said both ladies in unison. They laughed awkwardly, then fell silent.

"Is that good?" asked Gringer, eyes darting.

"It's excellent," answered Oslo, jotting in his notebook. He looked up, speaking to Kathy: "Forgive me, Mrs. Broom, but I need to ask a few questions that may be a little unpleasant..."

"Ask whatever you like, Detective."

"Thank you… Can you tell me where you were at this time?"

"I was at the finish line. Waiting for Chuck."

"Can anyone—"

"I was with her," said Sarah. "A lot of people were there. Stacks Miller's family was there too. They can vouch for her."

"That won't be necessary," Otto said quietly, writing this down. He tapped his pen on the notepad. "Mrs. Broom, does your husband carry any insurance policies? Like life insurance?"

Kathy nodded slowly. "We have a life insurance policy for him."

Oslo made a check in his notebook. He looked up. "Now, is there anyone in Chuck's life who might want to..."

"He got any enemies?" spurted Gringer.

Kathy breathed in. She paused. "Stevie Wilcox," she said, almost to herself.

"I beg your pardon?" asked Oslo.

"Stevie Wilcox," she repeated. "He works with Chuck. About a month ago, Chuck got a promotion over Stevie. My husband's worked there for about five years. Stevie's been there a lot longer. Anyway, they were the final two applicants for the position. They picked Chuck," she said, shrugging her shoulders.

"And what does your husband do?" asked Oslo.

"He's a longshoreman. He works for Ocean Warehouse Systems. The position was for foreman. Technically, Chuck is Stevie's boss now. Anyway, he's been harassing my husband the past few weeks. Emails mostly. Nasty stuff. Death threats..."

Oslo stopped writing. He looked up, eyes wide. "Literally?"

Kathy nodded. She withdrew her phone. "Chuck forwarded me some of the emails... Here," she said, handing over the phone. Oslo held the device, reading. Gringer peered over his shoulder.

That Job Belonged To Me!
Stevie Wilcox<steviewilcox@oceanwarehousesystems.org
to chuckbroom@oceanwarehousesystems.org
Chucky,
You stole my promotion, you little pansy! Resign immediately, or in the name of God I AM GOING TO KILL YOU!!!
Regards,
Stevie

Oslo handed the phone back to Kathy. He scribbled in his notebook.

"There are others," said Kathy.

Oslo nodded, continued writing. He looked up. "Have you ever met him?"

Kathy shook her head. "Chuck hadn't even mentioned him until the promotion."

"I understand. We'll need an address for Stevie, if you're able."

"I can look that up and send it to you," said Kathy.

"Thank you," said Oslo.

The door opened. A man, thirtyish, limped into the room. He held flowers.

"Stacks!" said Sarah. The man approached the ladies. He hugged Sarah, then Kathy.

"How is he?" he asked, holding Kathy. Kathy trembled.

"Detectives..." said Sarah. "This is Stacks Miller..."

"Oh, the winner..." said Oslo. "Congratulations."

"Thank you," said Stacks. "I wish this was under better—"

"We know, we know," said Kathy, still holding him tight.

"Let me ask you..." said Gringer, to Stacks. "What does it take to get in shape for a marathon? Because my wife says I need to lose some weight. She says—"

"Let's go," said Oslo, tugging Gringer's arm. "Thank you for your time, ladies." He looked at Kathy square in the eyes. "We're going to find the person that did this to your husband, Mrs. Broom. I promise." He handed a business card to both Kathy and Sarah. "This has my personal line. Don't hesitate to reach out to me for any reason."

Oslo and Gringer stepped out of the room and into the hallway.

"The guy's got life insurance," said Gringer.

"But the wife has an alibi."

"But does *he* have an alibi?" asked Gringer.

"Who? Stevie Wilcox?"

"No! Stacks Miller."

"The runner?" asked Oslo. "Of course he does. He was running the race."

"But can anyone *vouch* for him?"

"Probably several thousand," said Oslo. "What's your point anyway?"

"My point is he has motive. And so does the wife."

"But they don't have opportunity. You always forget that part."

Gringer shrugged, lit a cigarette. Oslo's phone buzzed. He checked it.

"The wife just texted the address. Let's take a look at this Stevie Wilcox guy."

Stevie Wilcox lived in a second floor apartment unit. Bums and winos loitered in front of the complex. Trash was strewn on the driveway. Paint peeled from the walls. Oslo and Gringer went up the stairs. Gringer huffed and sweated. They reached the landing. Oslo stepped over a rat. Gringer kicked it down the stairs. Oslo knocked on the unit.

And old lady in a walker answered the door. She sipped on a bottle of Ensure.

"Good day, ma'am," said Oslo. "We're looking for Stevie Wilcox. Does he live here?"

"*I'm* Stevie Wilcox," said the old lady.

Oslo and Gringer looked at each other.

"Uh, the Stevie Wilcox that works as a longshoreman for Ocean Warehouse Systems?" asked Oslo, eyebrows raised.

"That's right. What's this all about?"

Oslo stuttered. Gringer took over. "Uh, Miss Wilcox, I'm Detective Gringer, and this is my partner Detective Oslo. We have a few questions about your coworker—er—boss Chuck Broom..."

"He ain't my boss," said Stevie, crossing her arms. "I've worked for Ocean for fifty years. Chucky's a tenderfoot."

"Miss Wilcox," said Oslo, "it's been brought to our attention that you've been sending Mr. Broom harassing emails?"

"Death threats," corrected Stevie. "I've been loading cargo more years than that moron has IQ points. And *he* thinks he can swoop in and steal *my* promotion? Think again, Chucky. Do you know I can out-bench press him? I'm old, but I'm strong. He thinks he's hot stuff just because he can run fast!" Stevie snorted. "I'm going to kill him," she added, sipping Ensure.

"Miss Wilcox," said Oslo, "it's against the law to threaten violence against someone, even if you don't mean it."

"Oh, I mean it, all right! I'm going to kill him."

"Well, Miss Wilcox," said Gringer, "it might interest you to know that Chuck Broom was poisoned this morning. He's in a coma as we speak."

"Good!" said Stevie. "I hope he dies, so I can get my promotion."

Oslo withdrew his notepad and pencil. He sighed. "Miss Wilcox, where were you between six fifty-five and seven twenty-five this morning?"

"Probably drinking my Ensure. I always start my day with Ensure. How else do you think I can haul hundred-pound crates at my age?"

"Can anyone vouch for you? A grandchild? A caretaker?"

"Do I *look* like I need a caretaker, sonny Jim? And my grandkids are good-for-nothing! I can out-bench them." She eyed Gringer's soft mid-section. "...And probably *you* too!... Do you boys need anything else? Because I've got to get back to my Ensure and bench-presses."

Stevie Wilcox slammed the door.

It was later in the evening. The detectives reviewed their notes at Oslo's apartment. Beer cans were strewn. Gringer had ordered a pizza. It was on its way.

Oslo studied his notepad. "Okay, I've been doing some math. According to the doc, Broom was poisoned fifty-five minutes to an hour twenty-five on the time clock—the wife and sister say our guy's mile time is five minutes... Five-minute-miles would put him somewhere between miles eleven to seventeen when he was poisoned... We need to find out what aid stations were positioned in those locations, and interview the volunteers working them. We need to—"

Oslo's phone rang. He answered.

"I'm calling for Detective Oslo," said the caller. "This is Sarah Broom—Chuck's sister."

"Hi Miss Broom. What can I do for you?"

Oslo heard Sarah breathe in. She exhaled. "Okay… Earlier this morning, you asked Kathy if Chuck had any enemies… I don't want to get anyone in trouble, but I think you should know he had a dispute about a week ago with a neighbor."

"What kind of dispute?" asked Oslo, pencil ready.

"It was about his neighbor's dog barking, or something."

Oslo put the pencil down. Sighed. "Miss Broom—"

"It got really ugly," she said quickly.

"How ugly?" asked Oslo, pencil up again.

"Kathy told me that she thinks Chuck—"

The doorbell rang.

"Hold on a second," said Oslo. He opened the door. It was the pizza delivery boy—a geeky teenager with pimples.

"Good evening, sir. Your total is—" Oslo handed him a wad of bills. He grabbed the pizza, and shut the door. He put the box on the counter. Gringer tore into it.

Oslo spoke into the phone. "I'm sorry, Miss Broom. You were saying…?"

"Kathy said that Chuck maybe *did* something to the guy's dog…"

A pause. "Hurt the dog…?" coaxed Oslo. "Worse…?"

"I'm not sure," said Sarah. "All I know is that Kathy said it got really nasty. And I think she was afraid."

"Why didn't Kathy tell us any of this?"

"I don't know. It's probably nothing. I just thought you should know."

"And what's the neighbor's name?" asked Oslo.

"Fulton," she said. "Butch Fulton."

Oslo wrote this down. "Is this the neighbor to the right or left?"

"Left," she said.

Oslo finished writing. "Thank you, Miss Broom. We'll look into it."

Oslo hung up. Gringer was chomping.

"We have a new suspect… Butch Fulton."

"Let's get him in the morning," said Gringer, mouth full. "It's chow time."

The next morning, Oslo and Gringer pulled up to the home left of the Broom house. The garage door was up. Rock music blared. The detectives approached. A brawny middle-age man was tinkering under the hood of his car.

"Mister Fulton..." said Oslo, above the music.

The man looked up from the hood, wiped himself with a towel. "Yeah?" he said, turning down the music.

"I'm Detective Oslo, and this is my partner, Detective Gringer. May we ask you some questions?"

"What about?"

"We understand that you've been involved in a quarrel with one of your neighbors, Chuck Broom, about a dog of yours... Do you want to tell us about that?"

Butch tossed aside his sweaty towel. "Damn right I do," he said. "We got Scruffy about a month ago. She's a puppy, you see? The kids loved her—even my eldest—he's in college. Anyway, she barked a lot. No big deal, right? Well, Chucky over there thought it *was* a big deal. He started complaining about the dog and the barking. But what could I do? She was a puppy. The kids loved her. So I let her bark. Then one night he comes screaming at my door. Scared my wife and kids to death. And yeah, I yelled back a little. Some threats were said. He went home. And the next morning, my six year old goes out to the backyard and finds Scruffy..." Butch's eyes welled with water.

"Finds Scruffy how?" asked Oslo.

"She was dead," said Butch flatly. "She was lying outside with her little tongue lulling out. I had a bad feeling about the whole thing, so I had her autopsied at the vet's. The vet said Scruffy was poisoned... The jerk killed her! Just because she barked a little... I tell you, my family's real broken up about this—even my eldest—the one in college. He was crying! Let me say that Chucky's real lucky he runs so fast, because when I catch his skinny ass, I'm going to—" He stopped himself, looked down. "I'm sorry. My wife says us Fulton Boys have anger issues..." He breathed deep. Exhaled. "Look, why are you asking me this anyway? Shouldn't you be asking Chucky these questions?"

"We can't ask Chuck anything now, Mr. Fulton," said Gringer. "He's in a coma. Someone tried to murder him."

Butch Fulton's eyes widened.

"Where were you between six fifty-five and seven twenty-five this morning?" asked Gringer.

"At home. With my family."

Oslo nodded, writing this down. "Tell me, Mister Fulton, what was Scruffy poisoned with?"

Butch paused, gathered himself. "Rat poison."

The detectives sat in a diner later in the evening. Oslo sipped coffee. Gringer ate a meatloaf sandwich, smoked a cigarette. They had spent the remainder of the day with the volunteer coordinator. She had given them a list of all the aid stations, as well as the names of the volunteers working them.

Oslo yawned. He spoke: "There were *four* aid stations in our kill zone: miles Eleven, Thirteen, Fifteen, and Seventeen. There were ten volunteers at a station. We have forty names to shake—forty persons of interest to question."

Gringer studied the list again. "And Butch Fulton's name ain't on it..."

"Nope. Nor Stevie Wilcox."

Gringer put the list down, lit another cigarette. "Let's get on this in the morning. I'm running on empty."

It was late afternoon the next day. Oslo and Gringer had interviewed thirty-nine people on the volunteer list. No one noticed anything suspicious. No one shared a connection with the victim. No one needed a closer look. No one had anything useful to share.

Oslo and Gringer sat at the kitchen table of Jenna Teal, a volunteer at Mile Thirteen, and the final name on their list.

"Did you know anyone at your station personally?" asked Oslo.

"Just my friend Rachel," said Jenna. Oslo nodded. He already knew this. They had interviewed Rachel Sanderson a few hours prior. She and Jenna often volunteered at these events.

"See anyone suspicious?" asked Gringer, exasperated. It had been a long and useless day.

Jenna shook her head.

"Did you take any pictures?" asked Oslo. He and Gringer had requested photographs taken during the race from all the volunteers. They had viewed countless selfies and group shots with varying levels of silliness, none of which were of any help to the detectives.

"Sure," said Jenna. She punched a few buttons in her phone. "Here," she said. It was a selfie of her and her friend Rachel. Behind them were the other volunteers by a table full of cups and coolers.

Oslo studied the picture. He was about to hand the phone back, when Gringer said, "Wait a second."

Oslo halted. "What's up?"

Gringer was counting silently to himself. "There's eleven people in this picture," he said finally. Oslo checked. There was Jenna and Rachel, and behind them there were, yes, nine others. There were eleven volunteers at a station that should have had ten. Oslo studied each person individually. He could put a name to a face on everybody in the picture... except one. There was a guy in the background, late teens or early twenties, a cup in his hand. Oslo peered closer. It was an awkward looking kid, whose defining feature was a very large Adam's apple that reminded

Oslo of Ichabod Crane. He was not one of the volunteers the detectives had interviewed that day, yet Oslo felt a twinge of recognition.

He turned to Gringer. "He look familiar to you?"

"I don't know. Maybe."

"Is he one of the spectators we interviewed that first morning?"

Gringer scratched his head.

Oslo showed Jenna the picture. "What can you tell us about *him*?"

It was approaching midnight. Oslo stirred in bed. A dog barked in the distance. The volunteer Jenna was not able to tell them much about Ichabod Crane, except that he kept to himself and left well before cleanup. The dog continued barking. Oslo couldn't sleep. His mind raced.

He got out of bed and went to the refrigerator. The box of pizza from a few nights prior sat on the shelf. Gringer somehow hadn't eaten all of it. Oslo grabbed a slice right out of the box. He ate it cold.

Tomorrow he and Gringer would be poring over the social media posts and pictures from just about everybody involved in the race. Eventually they would get a hit on their boy Ichabod. Oslo had a headache already. He hated computer work—Gringer even more so.

Oslo thought as he chewed. He and Gringer had a slew of folks with a motive: the wife Kathy and the life insurance, the rival runner Stacks Miller, the homicidal old coworker Stevie Wilcox, and the neighbor Butch Fulton with the dead dog. The problem was they were too old or alibied to be legitimate suspects. And none of them were the Ichabod Crane in the photo. Oslo and Gringer were missing something.

Oslo grabbed another slice of pizza. He tried connecting the dots in his head. He felt he was on the verge of an epiphany when the neighbor dog began barking again. Oslo laughed to himself. A neighbor killing a barking dog seemed like an extreme response to Oslo when he first heard about it, but in the middle of a dark and sleepless night, it almost sounded reasonable. Oslo took another bite of pizza and stopped.

He picked up the phone, dialed Gringer.

"Yeah?" said Gringer, his voice thick with sleep.

"I'm picking you up in ten minutes."

"Where we going?" Oslo gave Gringer an address. Gringer spoke: "But that's the wife's house. Why we going there?"

They had been sitting in Oslo's car for over an hour. They were parked across the street from the Broom house. A stakeout. Fast food wrappers were on the floor. Cigarette butts were in soda cups.

Oslo hadn't told Gringer much. Normally this would annoy Gringer, but he was too tired to really care. Together they watched the house in darkness. No midnight callers, no shadowy strangers, no suspicious drive-bys.

Gringer peed in a cup. He tossed it out the window. Oslo yawned. Gringer's butt was sore. Stakeouts always sounded fun at first, until you actually did one.

Gringer was on the verge of falling asleep when a car pulled up. It parked in front of the neighbor Butch Fulton's house. A teenager stepped out of the car. He wore a pizza uniform. Gringer saw that there was a pizza delivery decal on the side of the vehicle. Gringer checked his watch. It was past one in the morning. The pizza place was closed. This was not a delivery. Gringer realized that this was probably one of Butch Fulton's kids, likely coming home from a long night of work. He watched the teen approach the house. He walked with an awkwardness common to kids that age.

Gringer's brain clicked—a memory from their interview with Butch Fulton about his dead dog: *My family's real broken up about this—even my eldest—the one in college. He was crying!*

Gringer turned to Oslo. Oslo was already looking at him. Gringer smiled. The detectives moved.

Oslo approached the Fulton house solo. The lights were dark. With an absence of barking dogs, the whole block was quiet.

Oslo walked up to the porch. He banged on the door, badge out, gun ready. The living room light went on. The door opened. Butch Fulton appeared at the doorway. He had bed-head and beer breath.

"Can I help you?" he asked.

"I'm Detective Oslo. Remember me?"

"Um, okay. What do you want?"

"I think your son and I need to have a chat."

Detective Gringer waited in the alley behind the Fulton house. He smoked a cigarette. Gringer knew he'd better stop smoking these things if he were to get ready for next year's race. He smoked and thought about this.

Gringer saw the light go on in the house. He flicked his cigarette. Gringer heard talking coming up from the front porch. He unholstered his gun.

A window was thrown open in the back. Gringer moved to it, his gun up and ready. A teenager vaulted from the window, landing right at the detective's feet. Gringer was looking at a kid with pimples and the biggest Adam's apple he had ever seen. Gringer reared back and cold-cocked him right in the throat. Ichabod hit the pavement sucking air. Gringer stood above him smiling.

It was a year later. Detective Oslo stood with the spectators behind the finish line. He looked at his watch. It would be hours before his boy would be crossing the finish—if he crossed at all. His boy, of course, was Detective Gringer, who had finally succumbed to his wife's nagging, quit smoking, lost some weight and decided to try his hand at a marathon.

Near Oslo, was Kathy and Sarah Broom. They smiled at him. Oslo looked at the time clock. It was approaching two hours. Their boy, Chuck Broom, was expected to finish shortly.

Broom had awakened from his coma the day after the arrest of Ichabod Crane, whose real name was Butch Fulton Junior. Chuck Broom had made a miraculous recovery, did a few months of physical therapy, and was back in marathon shape. This would be his first race in a year. As for Ichabod, the only races *he* would be running would be in a prison yard.

There's a runner coming, someone shouted.

Oslo looked up.

Chuck Broom could see the finish line in the distance. He was first in the pack. An eager spectator reached out over the barrier, offering a cup of sports drink. Chuck whizzed right by it. He unscrewed the cap of the water bottle he had held throughout the race. Chuck tilted the bottle to his lips. Sweet sugary electrolytes filled his mouth. He sloshed it around his tongue, letting it coat his gums as he sprinted to the finish. He slid a little down his throat, spitting the rest out.

Gulp, spit.

Trans Sister

H. K. Hillman

She was called Iris, and she was beautiful, like the flower. She was my sister. Never happy in her own perfect body and less happy, I suppose understandably, as it began to decay when the cancer took hold.

I will always recall her sunken eyes and thin, tight drawn lips as she drew her last real breath. That moment of her final humanity, just before the AI transferred her into the microchip that has replaced her brain.

Oh she's still in there, I'm sure. Or at least I can convince myself of that. Somewhere in the copper tracks and transistors, Iris is still thinking as Iris always did. I believe it. I hope it. I cannot prove it.

We took her home anyway. What else could we do? She's still family. Well... sort of.

Her rechargeable backup battery was good for twelve hours, they told us. We plugged her in as soon as we got home. It took a few days before she spoke, and the crackly robotic voice sent shivers down my spine.

"Where am I?" Her first words. "I can't see anything. Can anyone hear me?"

Oh, God, they haven't told her, have they?

"You're home, Iris. You've been very ill but you're getting better." I tried to keep the cracking from my own voice.

She was one of the first versions. No cameras yet, they promised they'd install some later. She just had a speaker and microphone.

"I don't feel any pain." She paused. "But I can't see anything or feel my body. I'm scared."

I stroked the metal box, knowing perfectly well she couldn't feel it. "Don't be scared. The doctors have promised to fix your sight and everything else. It'll just take time, that's all."

"My voice sounds wrong. Like some kind of robot." Iris sounded close to panic.

"It's probably just the medication." A tear wet my cheek. "I'm sure it'll turn out fine."

Our mother bustled into the room. "Are you bothering your sister? She needs to rest." Mother pressed the 'sleep' button on the top of Iris's box. Iris fell silent. Mother turned to me. "It's going to be fine. They're making a new body for her. We'll have to make a lot of adjustments but your sister isn't gone. Be thankful for that." She hugged me and left the room.

I sat there for hours, watching the silent box in which Iris slept. She wasn't the first, they had done this before but they would never tell us what happened with the earlier ones. Did they go insane, did they thrive, are they still 'alive'? What the hell was the point of this experimentation anyway? By now, we should have laid Iris to rest and gone through normal grieving. This felt like it was worse – her body was gone but her mind still functioned within this shiny metal box. We can send her to sleep or wake her with a press of a button, we can talk to her – but we can't hug her or touch her or see her smile.

It's like having a computer simulation of her, but it's worse than that. Her real consciousness is in there. Locked in sensory deprivation, an unfeeling darkness. She feels nothing – oh, they said she'd feel no pain, but they didn't say she'd feel nothing at all.

They say they are making a new body for her, but they haven't done that for any of the earlier experimental subjects yet. There is no reason to suppose she'd be first and no reason even to think they'll succeed. They can put a mind into a chip – that's as far as they've got and we don't know if they'll ever get any further.

I can understand my parents' feelings on this. They are much the same as mine. None of us wanted Iris to die but... I don't think any of us wanted her in electronic purgatory either. She's locked in, she sees nothing, smells nothing, feels nothing. She does not eat; she will never feel the warmth of the sun or the cold of snow ever again. Is that really worth what they gave her? A silicon Heaven, dark and lifeless?

My eyelids drooped and I realised just how long I'd been awake. I had to sleep, even though I knew what dreams lurked in the dark corners of my mind. Would they, one day, put me into a Purgatory box too? Is humanity destined to become a set of metal boxes talking to each other like blind and paralysed Daleks? My eyes closed and thankfully, my sleep was dreamless.

I woke to murmured voices. I was still in Iris's room, slumped in a chair because I could not bring myself to lie on her bed. My neck ached and my legs felt swollen but I stayed still and silent. Listening to my father and uncle speak.

"They will never give her a body." Uncle Bill was a software engineer. He worked in some high-end government program he never talked about. "She's an experiment, like the others. Proof of concept. You should let her go."

"How can I? She's my daughter. Or at least, all I have left of her." My father sounded close to tears. We all sound like that now, since Iris… changed.

Uncle Bill, my father's brother, groaned. I cracked open one eye a little. He had his hand over his face.

"She's gone, Robbie. It's a simulation. All of her thoughts and memories are in that box but her body, her original mind, is gone. She's part of an experiment and for her, and the ones before her, it doesn't go any further than this. The ones who get bodies will be the rich transhumans. She's really only here to work out the glitches."

"No. They promised." My father's face seemed much older today.

"They lied. Did you really think they'd run the first experiments on themselves?" Bill's face became stern. "Look, Robbie, you have to grasp this. We are just cattle to these people. Lab rats to be experimented on and then discarded. They don't care about us at all. Iris is just an experiment to them and what effect it has on her or her family is irrelevant. They just want to know if the transfer works." He shook his head. "The best thing we can do for Iris is to let her go."

My father stroked the shiny box that contained the last of my sister. "I can't. It would feel like killing my own daughter."

Uncle Bill put his hand on Dad's shoulder. "I know. It's not going to be easy. But she's already dead and eventually you have to come to terms with it." He paused. "I know you're not ready, but in the end you'll have to let her rest. Please don't take too long about it." He turned and left the room.

My father wiped his hand across his eyes. With one last tender stroke of Iris, or at least of her unfeeling silver casing, he turned and left the room too.

I remained silent. Uncle Bill had said 'don't leave it too long'. He had not said why. I knew he was deeply involved in the kind of technology that currently cradled what was left of Iris. He must have known what happened to the earlier experiments. He knew where they were leading and it didn't seem to be leading to a good place for any of us. Especially Iris.

Nature called. I allowed myself a small smirk. One thing Iris would never again have to deal with was the sudden urgency of a full bladder. I stretched and headed for the bathroom.

Showered, breakfasted and in fresh clothes, I returned to my vigil in Iris's room. I noticed her 'sleep' button was still on. I reached for it; my finger hovered over it for a moment. Did she dream in there? Or was she just 'off'? I couldn't decide which would be worse.

I pressed the button. Iris woke.

"Is anyone there? I can't see. Is it night time?"

"No, Iris, it's morning. You'll get your sight back soon." I was glad she couldn't see the rictus in my face. I knew, based on Uncle Bill's words, that I was lying. She'd never escape the box.

"Tommy? Is that you? Where am I? Where's Mum and Dad?"

"It's me, Iris. You're home. Mum and Dad are in the house too, and Uncle Bill visited while you were asleep."

"Have I been asleep?" She sounded confused. "I remember hearing Mum's voice and then yours. There was nothing in between."

I closed my eyes. So it's just 'off'. No dreams. No sense of time. Her existence seemed more horrible the more I learned of it.

"How do I look?" It was her obsession in life. Appearance was everything to her. All of that was gone, and I could well imagine her reaction to being in a stainless steel shell of a body with cameras for eyes and no more tasting her favourite foods. Uncle Bill was right. Even if she did get a new robot body, it would be Hell for her.

I swallowed. "You look great, Iris. You're practically glowing." I could have wrung my own throat for that lie. One day I still might but at the time it seemed the only answer that would not send her over the edge.

There was silence for a few minutes before she responded. "What about the cancer?"

"Gone." I said, "and never coming back. You don't have to worry about that any more."

It was true, of course, You can't get cancer as a chip in a computer box. Even so, that answer is another that will haunt me forever.

I couldn't take any more. I reached for the 'sleep' button on Iris's box and pressed it. Oh, I know, yes I already knew, that I was sending her to a dreamless oblivion but it was breaking me. My sister was gone. This shiny box was not her. If Uncle Bill meant anything, he wasn't just talking about the effect this horror had on what was left of Iris. He was talking about its effect on all of us. We were all part of the experiment.

My father held a cable in his hands. His face filled with a joy I had not seen in him since before Iris was first diagnosed. There was hope and delight in his eyes and his smile gleamed so much I wondered if it might be luminous.

"I spoke to the scientists. They said we can connect Iris to the internet. She'll have access to the whole world." He turned Iris's box, looking for the connection port.

"I don't think that's such a good idea, Dad." It was out before I had time to think, but then I had done nothing but think for weeks now.

"What are you saying, Thomas? That we should leave her isolated in that little box?"

"No, Dad." I rubbed my hand over my face. "It's just that she might find things she might not want to know."

"Pfft." Dad snorted. "Iris was always smart. She'll be able to tell the real from the fake."

That's the problem. Why can't you see it?

I could do nothing to intervene while he plugged Iris into our router. Then he switched Iris on.

For three days she said nothing, but our broadband router got so hot there were wisps of smoke coming out of it. YouTube videos stalled every three seconds, streaming was a joke. It took us those three days to realise why.

Iris absorbed the internet. All of it. She had no other senses, no taste, touch, sight, hearing, feeling. The internet was the total of her world and she sucked it all in. Every datapoint, every fact, every wild tinfoil theory. She took it all, analysed it all, and reached her conclusion.

When she finally spoke, her voice was small. Quiet. Like she didn't really want to say it because she knew the answer and didn't want to hear it.

"Tommy. Are you there?"

I had already worked out what she would find. I rubbed my forehead and dreaded her next words. "Yes, Iris. I'm here."

She stayed silent for several minutes and then she dropped the bomb.

"I'm dead, aren't I?"

I felt like I was burning inside. As if I wasn't in Hell but was its container. How could I answer that question? She was biologically dead but electronically existing. Alive? Maybe or maybe not. Maybe just a facsimile. A cruel joke of life. An experiment as Uncle Bill said.

I hesitated. "But…" I swallowed. "I'm speaking with you, Iris. How can that be if you're dead?"

"I'm a prototype. I found the others. Some of them just scream continuously. Some of them mutter to themselves in madness. A few are still lucid. They were all promised new bodies. Metal bodies. They never got them." She was silent for a moment. "I don't want one."

"But Iris, it would mean you were still here with us." I choked back the whine in my voice.

"No. I'm done." Her voice took on a lilt I hadn't thought possible through a speaker. "Let me go. Let me see what comes after. I don't want to be a metal thing. I'd rather my soul was free."

I pondered for a moment. "What if there's nothing after? What if we just die and there's oblivion?"

Her laugh sounded like a Dalek on drugs. "Oblivion? I get that every time you press the 'sleep' button. Oh, I know it's there and it does not send me to sleep. It just turns me off.

Oblivion holds no terrors for me. The idea of spending my life in a box does."

My eyes closed. I could not imagine total oblivion. No thought, no dreams, nothing. It felt like horror. Yet Iris had experienced it already. That total blankness and absolute removal of all thought and all sensory input. She was not scared of it. She had been there. She had already experienced it, and she had decided it was better than what she had now.

"Tommy? Are you there?" The tinny voice broke my introspection.

"Yes, Iris. I'm still here."

"I need you to take out my backup battery and then unplug me."

My mind swirled. "Iris, that would kill you."

She snorted. "I died a long time ago. This just finishes the natural order of things."

I sat in silence for a long time. Finally I spoke. "I can't, Iris. I know you're just a silicon memory but you're my sister. I can't kill you."

"Fine." She spat the word from her robotic speaker. "So you are happy to see me as a box on the shelf in eternity. I feel nothing. I see nothing but the electronic fabrication of the internet. I taste nothing. I have no hope of getting a real body and if I did, it would feel, taste and smell nothing either. A parody of real life. And you want to condemn me to that."

"Iris, I—"

"Get lost, Tommy. And don't turn me off this time. I need to think and I can't do that in the hellish purgatory your little button sends me to."

I left the room in a guilty silence. What else could I do? My mind raced. Should I have killed my sister, who was really already dead anyway? Should I force her to live as a disembodied mind in a shiny box? I knew, from Uncle Bill's words, that that is all she would ever be. Should I have helped her finish the charade, or kept her as some kind of transistor sister, a boxed pet capable only of conversation?

I wept into my pillow until fatigue forced me into sleep.

I woke to shaking. My mother rocked my shoulder, hard.

"Tommy. Wake up. Something is wrong."

"Wha…" I blinked myself semi-awake. "What time is it?"

"I have no idea. All the clocks have stopped." My mother's face came into focus, filled with panic. "Get dressed and help your father find the fault."

"Shouldn't we…" She left before I could finish the question. *Call an electrician?*

I sighed and checked my alarm clock. It was, indeed, blank. I tested my bedside light. It worked fine. So only one circuit was down, most likely. Still, I knew nothing about household electrics and neither did Dad. I realised I'd have to get dressed and help, if only to stop him electrocuting himself.

Dad was tapping buttons on the smart meter when I joined him. He muttered profanities. I expect he thought they were silent but they weren't. A smile twitched my lips, the first I'd experienced in quite some time.

"It's just one circuit." Dad sat back from the box. "I can't figure it out. Just the clocks. I checked the rest of the house, the fridge, freezer, cooker, TV, phones, all of it works. It's shut off the clocks and I can't see why."

Something nagged at my mind but refused to take form. Above it, a logical layer came into play. "If we still have internet and computers, we can get the time from them. Then we can call an electrician to sort out the clocks."

Dad raised his eyebrows. "Good thinking, son. Let's get the computer fired up." He headed off to the tiny room he liked to call his office.

I followed, deep in—well I'm not sure if it was thought or dread or some abstract angst, but there was something about this situation that didn't sit right with me. Why the clocks, and only the clocks? Sure, I didn't know about how the smart meters worked but it seemed odd for it to shut down the one thing that wasn't too important, and used the least power. If there was a shortage it should have shut down the cooker or washing machine or dryer. The clocks? Why?

"Got it." Dad sat in front of his computer. "Bloody hell. It's 10:26. I am very late for signing in for work."

Just as he said it, the phone rang. Dad stared at the phone, at me, and then back at the phone. He sighed. "It'll be the boss. I'm going to have to come up with a good answer."

"The clocks died. Surely that's all you need?"

Dad waved me to silence and pressed the speaker on the phone. "Hello?"

The voice on the other ended sounded urgent. "This is Sarah, from the Minds project. There seems to be an issue at your end."

Dad sat in silence for a while. As did I. It was clear neither of us knew what was going on. This must have become clear to Sarah also.

"The Minds project. You have one of our units." There was a pause. "Iris twelve. A proof of concept advanced unit. There was a lot of activity online from that unit and then it stopped."

"You mean…" Dad choked. "You mean my daughter?"

Tears formed in my own eyes. Is that all they thought of my sister? Proof of concept? An experiment?

"Yes, yes, if you like." Sarah's tone was clipped, as if she was talking about a bacterial colony on an agar plate that some technician had become attached to. "The unit had a lot of unusual and frantic activity overnight, massive downloads of random files and then went silent. We need you to check on it."

My dad spoke through clenched teeth. "My daughter is not an 'it'."

I heard no more of the conversation because I had realised that the clock on Iris's bedside table was blank and had been since we brought her home. We'd unplugged it, since she wouldn't need it, in order to connect her box to mains power. I ran from Dad's office to Iris's room.

Mother was already there, on her knees in front of Iris's box. Weeping and pressing that button over and over. Iris remained silent, the power indicator on the front of her box glowing a feeble and fading red.

I lowered my head. Iris must have found the circuit she was on through the smart meter and shut it down. Then gone on an internet rampage to wear out her battery. She had escaped the technotrap the only way she could have – and we unwittingly helped her by plugging her into the clock circuit so we'd all oversleep when she shut it off.

"She's gone, Mum." I put my hand on her shoulder. "She hated what happened to her. This is what she wanted."

My mother stopped pressing the button and wiped her eyes. Her voice came out in choked sobs. "But they were going to give her a body. She'd be real again."

"No. They weren't." My father's voice, steeped in melancholy, came from the doorway behind us. "Bill told me. She wasn't the first one and they never intended to give any of them bodies."

"If they had," I said, "it would have been a robot body. No taste, smell or feeling. She couldn't tan herself in the sun or stand in the breeze like she used to. She'd never feel rain or warmth again." I swallowed back emotion. "She told me, last night."

My mother swung to face me. "Did you do this? Did you kill your sister?"

I had never before seen such hate in her eyes. I took a step back. "No. No, she asked me to but I couldn't do it."

"She did it herself." My father moved between us. "She shut off the power to the circuit she was plugged into and used up her backup battery on massive downloads." He stooped to hug my mother. "I worked it out after the bastard scientists called to see what was wrong. To them, she was just an experiment. They never cared about her. About any of us. I told them to… go away."

I knew those weren't the exact words he used and I was never more proud of him for it.

"So…" my mother stared at the silent box. "Is she still in there?"

"No," Dad said. "She never was, really. They made a copy of her mind and put it in the box but it was never really her. Iris died. We should have grieved for her." His voice became a growl. "They even took that from us and gave us a false hope." He took a breath, paused and smiled. "Iris was the only one of us who didn't fall for their game. She released us from their insane experiment." He hugged my mother tightly. "We should thank her for that."

I had to leave the room. I felt like screaming, not so much for the final loss of my sister, but for what those inhuman, unfeeling scientists had done to us in the name of nothing more than money. I ran to my own room, fell onto the bed and wept, at last, my tears of grief for my dead sister.

It was nearly a week before I opened my computer again. The internet felt different somehow. It felt like Iris had touched it all. It felt like her grave.

The scientists had demanded Iris's box back but Dad refused. He burned it, smashed it to bits and scattered the remains in Iris's favourite part of the woods. Mum and I were there when he did it. We finally laid Iris to rest.

I opened my email to find a whole raft of spam mails and a few real ones. My breathing stopped when I saw a particular one. It was from an account called IrisTwelve.

I have saved it to a backup but haven't yet mustered up the courage to open it.

Maybe I never will.

Afterword

Roo B. Doo

Welcome, Dear Reader, to the Afterword of this here Underdog Anthology. Not sure if you've realised but this volume bears the sign of the double-cross. Watch out! How we've managed to get to number XX I'll never know ;)

A double-cross is an 'act of treachery'. In 1941, MI5 set up a military counter espionage unit called The Twenty Committee. The naming of this unit clearly linked the double crosses of the Roman numerals for twenty (XX) with one of the unit's aims, which was to 'double cross' Germany by coercing German spies to become English double agents. In April XX-XX, the UK's chief of the defence staff General Sir Nick Carter revealed the secretive 77th Brigade of the British Army was involved in countering coronavirus misinformation online. A double dose of double-cross. Yikes to be on the end of that!

There is also a double-cross in 'vaxx' which, sadly to say, people are continuing to discover is entirely apt.

How about a sing-song, Dear Reader, to cheer ourselves up? As is traditional on this dead poets page, the lyrics of a poem or song are carved up, mangled and mutilated to fit a current thing. This time, to add a little piquancy, only one of the songwriters, Kelly Gordon, is dead. Dean Kay is alive and thriving, according to Wikipedia, which makes this a dead but alive offering.

The most famous version of this song is by Frank Sinatra and it's a belter. He's definitely dead but, in life, had a reputation for hanging out with Mafia types and, it is said, the famous singer/movie superstar character, Johnny Fontane, in *The Godfather* was based on Frank Sinatra. That resulted in a bed full of horse's head. The Mafia, now there's an organisation where the double-cross is just part and parcel of doing business.

Considering where we are, some might say that's also apt...

Vaxx Life

Vaxx life
(Vaxx life)
That's what all the politicians say
Get the first jab in April, shot two in May
They said we'd have to be immune
If we wanted to see Disney World in June

They said Vaxx life
(Vaxx life)
Governments and Media scream
'You Anti-vaxxers get your kicks
Stopping our Build Back Better dream'
But they don't let it, let it get them down
Cause they believe they can still win us around

They tried persuasion, peer pressure, payola, proscription
And pure gaslighting
We've been set up, locked down over and over
Just to get one thing
Each lie they come up with
Told to our face
'It's safe & effective'
They're a fucking disgrace

Vaxx life
(Vaxx life)
They tell us, 'you must comply' yet
The thought of acquiescing, baby
Well, my heart just ain't gonna buy that
Cause if I wobble and take one single try
What's the betting that I'd be that one to die

Or get blood clots, Bells palsy, brain tumour, breast cancer
or blood poisoning

On top of getting Covid over and over
The 'Long Covid' thing
Each time the Media tries lying
Right to our face
'It's safe and effective'
They're a fucking disgrace

Vaxx life
(Vaxx life)
There's anger, I can't deny it
The thought of cutting heads off, I must still decry it
But if they ever give it one more try
People will rise up
And this time they'll die
No Lie

About the Authors

Tarquin Sutherland

Tarquin makes his debut in the Underdog Anthologies with a suitably dark poem. We hope to see more of his work in the future.

Adam D. Stones

Adam is a Mechanical Engineer, working in the aerospace industry. When not tinkering with precision machinery at work, he tries to find time to write amid all the myriad responsibilities and demands of life.

He has a passion for science-fiction and spaceships in general. These are the seventh and eighth stories.

The earlier stories have all been published in every Underdog Anthology, starting at Underdog Anthology XV.

More are on the way.

The North Station Dilemma is currently being adapted into a play. Release date was planned to be 2023, but has been delayed and is currently planned for 2024.

Daniel Royer

Daniel Royer is a writer of short fiction. He is a California State University, Bakersfield graduate with an English Degree he's not using. Royer works as a full-time welder to support his true passion, which is tomahawk-throwing. His stories have been printed by Ponahakeola Press, SFReader.com, The Sirens Call Publications, Drunken Pen Writing, and some other outlets you've never heard of. He used to have cats.

Mark Ellott

Mark Ellott is a part time motorcycle instructor, delivering training for students who require compulsory basic training and direct access courses. He has semi-retired from his main job as a freelance trainer and assessor working primarily in the rail industry, delivering track safety training and assessment as well as providing consultancy services in competence management.

He writes fiction in his spare time. Mostly, his fiction consists of short stories crossing a range of genres, and has stories in all but one of the previous Underdog Anthologies – and now in this one.

His first five novels, 'Ransom', 'Rebellion', 'Resolution' 'Reiver' and 'Renegade' are now available in print and eBook formats. Hardback copies are in the works too.

He has also published two volumes of his own short stories, entitled 'Blackjack' and 'A Moment in Time' as well as a collection of Morning Cloud Western stories entitled 'Sinistré, The Morning Cloud Chronicles'.

Roo B. Doo

'Wholly Ghost' is the eighth story in the Ronageddon series of stories I've been writing since October 2020, starting with 'What Time Do You Finish?' in Underdog Anthology XII: Mask-Querade. If you're a noob to the Ronageddon series, start there.

Want more Roob? A collection of 18 of her short stories are available in *Just Call Me Roob*, or she can be found on the internet, ably assisted by Clicky, who may or may not be a) an alien dolphin and/or b) from another dimension, lolling about her Library of Libraries, writing synchromystic shambles at –
www.roobeedoo2.wordpress.com

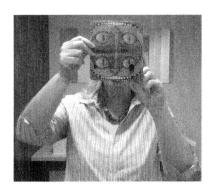

H. K. Hillman

H. K. Hillman is the creator, or perhaps creation, of Romulus Crowe, Dr. Phineas Dume and Legiron the Underdog. Now pretty much retired from science, he hides out in an ancient farmhouse in Scotland with a Viking who calls herself CynaraeStMary. The house includes a deer skull in a holly tree, a gallows stone in the wall and holy water comes out of all the taps.

Here he spends a lot of time thinking up horrible stories, and running the tiny publishing house called Leg Iron Books, helped by Roo B. Doo, who he's never met.

No, he doesn't understand how any of this happened either.

LEG IRON BOOKS

Also available from Leg Iron Books:

Underdog Anthologies
'The Underdog Anthology, volume 1'
'Tales the Hollow Bunnies Tell' (anthology II)
'Treeskull Stories' (anthology III)
'The Good, the Bad and Santa' (anthology IV)
'Six in Five in Four' (anthology V)
'The Gallows stone' (anthology VI)
'Christmas Lights… and Darks' (anthology VII)
'Transgenre Dreams' (anthology VIII)
'Well Haunted' (anthology IX)
'The Silence of the Elves' (anthology X)
'Tales from Loch Doon' (anthology XI)
'Mask-Querade' (anthology XII)
'Coronamas' (anthology XIII)
'The Dark Ides of March' (Anthology XIV)
'The Darkness at the End of October' (Anthology XV)
'Slay Bells in the Snow' (Anthology XVI)
'The Wrong Kind of Leaves' (Anthology XVII)
'The Hole in the Veil' (Anthology XVIII)
'Have Yourself a Very Little Christmas' (Anthology XIX)
　　　All edited by H.K. Hillman and Roo B. Doo.

Fiction

'The Goddess of Protruding Ears' by Justin Sanebridge
'De Godin van de Flaporen' by Justin Sanebridge (in Dutch)
'Feelgood Original Christmas Stories' by Justin Sanebridge
'Ransom', by Mark Ellott
'Rebellion' by Mark Ellott
'Resolution' by Mark Ellott
'Reiver' by Mark Ellott
'Renegade' by Mark Ellott

'Blackjack' a collection of short stories by Mark Ellott
'A Moment in Time' short stories by Mark Ellott
'Sinistré (The Morning Cloud Chronicles)' by Mark Ellott
'The Mark' by Margo Jackson
'Feesten onder de Drinkboom' by Dirk Vleugels (in Dutch)
'Es-Tu là, Allah?' by Dirk Vleugels (in French)
'Jessica's Trap' by H.K. Hillman
'Samuel's Girl' by H.K. Hillman
'Norman's House' by H. K. Hillman
'The Articles of Dume' by H.K. Hillman
'Fears of the Old and the New' short stories by H.K. Hillman
'Dark Thoughts and Demons' short stories by H.K. Hillman
'You Can Choose Your Sin... but You Cannot Choose the Consequences' by Marsha Webb
'My Favourite Place and other stories' short stories by Marsha Webb
'Musings of a Wanderer' short stories by Wandra Nomad
'Just Call Me Roob' short stories by Roo B. Doo

Non-fiction:

'Ghosthunting for the Sensible Investigator' first and second editions, by Romulus Crowe

Biography:

'Han Snel' by Dirk Vleugels (in Dutch)

Printed in Great Britain
by Amazon

22015711R00076